SONG
OF THE
GARGOYLE

Also by Zilpha Keatley Snyder

Featuring the Stanley Family
The Headless Cupid
The Famous Stanley Kidnapping Case
Blair's Nightmare
Janie's Private Eyes

And Condors Danced
Black and Blue Magic
The Changeling
The Egypt Game
Libby on Wednesday
Season of Ponies
Squeak Saves the Day
The Truth About Stone Hollow
The Velvet Room
The Witches of Worm

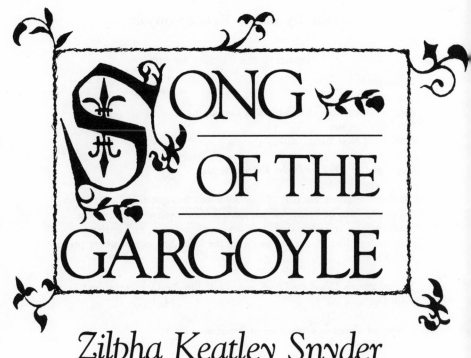

SONG OF THE GARGOYLE

Zilpha Keatley Snyder

Delacorte Press

Published by
Delacorte Press
Bantam Doubleday Dell Publishing Group, Inc.
666 Fifth Avenue
New York, New York 10103

Library of Congress Cataloging in Publication Data
Snyder, Zilpha Keatley.
    Song of the gargoyle / by Zilpha Keatley Snyder.
        p.   cm.
    Summary: When mysterious men in black abduct his father, the court jester of Austerneve, thirteen-year-old Tymmon flees into the forest, where he acquires a strange animal companion and plots to rescue his father.
    ISBN 0-385-30301-7
    [1. Adventure and adventurers—Fiction.]   I. Title.
PZ7.S68522So   1991   90-3772
[Fic]—dc20   CIP
                                                                              AC

Design by Paul Zakris
Manufactured in the United States of America
April 1991
10 9 8 7 6 5 4 3 2 1
BVG

To Larry

ONE

I t was well after midnight on a chill, dim night in early spring, and beneath a cloud-haunted sky Austerneve Castle slept deeply and heedlessly. In the castle's many chambers, in rooms large and small, on hard, narrow pallets and in grand canopied beds, bodies lay limply and minds drifted deep in dream. Even at the great gate the sentinels slumped at their posts. And in the tiny guardhouse beside the postern gate two aged watchmen rested their old heads on a table amid scattered chess pieces and snored peacefully.

Far up in the northwest tower, in a large round room that had once been a sentinels' wardroom, a boy of scarcely thirteen years was also sound asleep. Tymmon, son of Komus, the court jester of Austerneve, was sleeping peacefully and well, until he was awakened by a mysterious sound.

Startled wide awake as suddenly as if shaken by an unseen hand, Tymmon was not sure what he had heard. At
that moment of waking he only knew that there had been
a sound, and that its blurred echoes were still throbbing
through his sleep-clouded mind. It was only later, perhaps, in memory, that it seemed to have been a voice
calling his name from a great distance.

"Tymmon," a far faint voice might have cried. "Wake
up, Tymmon. They are coming."

But he could not be certain. Memories do tend to
shrink over time, and perhaps it followed that some of
them might grow instead—in new and important directions. And there had been moments when Tymmon had
wondered how much he remembered clearly of that
strange awakening. Perhaps, in the long hours that followed, his memory of that awful night *had* been shaped
and slanted by dreams.

"Too much of your life is dream-patterned," his father
had once told him. "You fool yourself with your dreaming." Tymmon had frowned, and as he often did, his father softened his scolding by making a jest of it. Crossing
his eyes and lolling his tongue, he did one of his comical
loose-legged capers and then, bending down to Tymmon's
height, went on. "We whose lives depend on fooling cannot afford to fool ourselves."

Komus's words had angered Tymmon, and he had
thought of saying, *"Your* life, Father, not *mine."* But biting
his tongue, he had only muttered, "My dreams are not of
fooling." Which, of course, meant much the same—if
Komus had been listening.

But one thing was certain. It had been a strange sound,

faint but clear, that had roused him that night during the dark, still hours before dawn. And it was also certain that the course of his life had been changed forever by that awakening.

At first he only sat up in bed, his heart racing and his breath coming in short gasps, as if he had just returned from the depths of some terrible nightmare, although he had no memory of such a dream. It was only the sound that he remembered—and the mysterious sense of grief and loss that followed it.

Crossing himself, he muttered a paternoster before he put aside the heavy sheepskin coverlet and rose to his feet. For a moment only he paused again, listening intently, but the call, if there had been one, did not repeat itself. He was calm now, his heart no longer racing, and it seemed to be only a vague uneasy curiosity that made him move forward through the inky darkness, feeling his way along the wall. He passed the hearth, where buried coals still glowed faintly from beneath the ash, and then circled out around the curtained bed where his father was still sleeping, breathing deeply and evenly.

There he lay, Komus, sound asleep in the fine four-poster bed that had been a gift from King Austern—a magnificent bed, draped and curtained like a stage. Tymmon silently pulled back the bed curtain and gestured grandly as if the bed were indeed a stage and as if he were presenting its occupant to an admiring audience.

Step up and feast your eyes, ladies and gentlemen. Here lies Komus, world-famous jester in the court of King Austern—and even more greatly famed as the honored sire of Tymmon the Great.

He grinned—mocking himself and his wild dreams of glory. For the truth of the matter was, of course, that Komus was not really famous. At least not outside of Austerneve, and even there one could hardly say that he was honored. Well known, perhaps, but hardly honored. Not as a clown and jester—a buffoon who earned his bread by making himself ridiculous. And certainly not honored for being the father of Tymmon, who was not great or famous either. Or—to put it more fairly—not *yet* great. Not yet great, perhaps, but one who did have plans. And dreams, if you will. Glorious dreams of . . .

A sudden realization that his feet on the stone floor were becoming as cold as the stones themselves interrupted Tymmon's musing. Silently replacing the curtain, he moved on around the bed and back to the wall, to follow its curve to where his groping fingers found the first of the hand- and toeholds that led up to the lookout window.

There were four of the high windows in the old wardroom—east, west, north, and south. Long ago they had been connected by a scaffolding, and a member of the palace guard had manned the lookout day and night to spy out the approach of dangerous visitors. Such careful watches had been necessary then, when it had been the custom for noble neighbors to pay murderous visits on each other's towns and castles. But now, with the North Countries long united under the peaceful reign of the High King, such precautions were no longer needed. And so the scaffolding and the ladder that led up to it had rotted away, and now no one could reach the window ledges.

No one, that is, except Tymmon himself, and he only this west ledge where age and erosion had made an ascent possible if one was young and agile and adept at finding toe- and fingerholds in the chinks and crannies of the old stone wall.

From long practice he found the footholds easily, and a moment later he was stretched out on the deep window ledge, peering down into the castle's courtyard far below. The window ledge, padded with goatskins and old cloaks, had long been one of his favorite hideaways, a place to read or dream or look down unseen on courtyard comings and goings—at the bustle of market on Saturday mornings, the drill of the palace guards on Wednesdays or, during almost any hour of the day, at his onetime friend, Lonfar, playing at jousting with the other pages.

Or when he tired of watching such childish games, he could turn and look the other way. Secretly look down into the one large room that was his home. The old guards' room at the top of the northwest tower, which had been granted to Komus free and clear for his lifetime by King Austern IX, ruler of Austerneve, the most ancient and honored kingdom of all the North Countries.

So what had once been a lookout window was still a spy hole in a way. In Tymmon's own private way, where, lying flat and still on the high ledge, he could not only spy on the castle courtyard but even on his own home and hearth—and sometimes watch his unsuspecting father do silly, private things. Such things as preening before a looking glass.

One had to admit that Komus the jester was a fine-featured man—when he wasn't twisting his face into a silly, stupid mask. Indeed, a handsome man, though not especially tall or stalwart or quite as comely, of course, as his young son, Tymmon. But his thatch of gold-brown hair was still thick and curly, his blue eyes wide and clear, his mouth well shaped, and his whole visage pleasant to look upon. That was a fact widely recognized, and recognized also by Komus himself—judging by the amount of time he spent before the glass.

At other times Tymmon had watched his father practicing some new bit of foolish prattle. Some witty bit of nonsense that was no doubt meant to burst forth as if unplanned and unprepared—to the amazement and amusement of King Austern and his guests.

Tymmon had watched from the window many times as his father preened and prattled. Watched secretly and unseen, hidden from view by the wide sill, even when daylight was streaming down above and around him. And so the window hideaway had remained his own private secret. Or so Tymmon had always thought—until that night. Until the night when . . .

Far below, the castle grounds were barely visible in the cloud-filtered moonlight. After he had made certain that there was nothing stirring in the courtyard to have caused the noise that awakened him, Tymmon turned away from the barred window and looked back down into the room below.

In the heavy, solid darkness of the tower room he could see nothing at all. But he was still seeing it in memory, remembering all the times he had spied on his father, when suddenly there was another sound. Not an indefinite blurry echo this time but an unmistakable clamor that clearly was not dreamt or imagined. A scuffling, thudding, clinking noise that seemed to come from the stone stairway that wound around the tower and ended at the wardroom door.

As Tymmon listened in dumb amazement, and with a growing sense of alarm, the sound grew quickly louder and then burst into a terrifying crescendo as the door flew open under a rain of heavy blows. Crouching low on the window ledge, he peered down into a scene of wild confusion and only stifled a cry of fear by pressing his hand across his mouth.

There were five of them, five huge men, armed and armored, their faces hidden by visored helmets. Two of them held great torches that filled the guardroom with a flickering red light, and all of them carried broadswords or daggers whose sharp blades reflected the torchlight like smaller tongues of fire. Charging into the room, upsetting chairs and the desk that held Komus's precious hoard of books and manuscripts, they spread out into a semicircle around a heavy-bodied man in a snouted black helmet who seemed to be their leader. The heavy man was shouting, but the words, echoing inside his helmet, came out in blurred fragments, without sense or meaning.

The muffled voice was still roaring when the bed curtains were thrown aside and Komus appeared in their midst. Komus, in his old ragged nightshirt, his hair wild and tangled, his face pale and tense in the flickering torchlight. Standing now only a pace away from the huge armored leader of the intruders, he looked, in comparison, pitifully small and frail—with his wide eyes and tousled hair, more like a slightly worn and weathered child than a full-grown man. The shouting stopped abruptly and for a moment the armored men stood still, turning their great metallic heads toward their leader and then back again toward Komus.

"Well, well, gentlemen." Komus was playing one of his jester roles, using a high-pitched and shaky voice, as he often did when he was miming fear in order to flatter some member of the court who liked to think of himself as particularly fierce and alarming.

"Well, well, gentlemen. To what do I owe this honor? Is it a celebration? A festive pilgrimage, perhaps? Here, let me offer a toast to whatever rite we are observing. A goblet of wine perhaps, all around." He bowed low, gesturing toward the wine barrel, but when he stepped toward it, the black-helmeted knight's gloved hand shot out and seized him by the arm.

"Enough of your nonsense, fool." The voice still held a ringing echo, like the fading notes of a brass gong, but now in the silence the strange sounds clumped themselves into recognizable words—cold, threatening words that seemed to throb not only in Tymmon's ears but also in the pit of his stomach. "You are to come with us, fool. You and your son, also." The gleaming angular head swung slowly from side to side. "Where is he? Where is the boy?"

On the high ledge Tymmon sank lower, pressing his body back against the window bars.

"I am to come with you?" Komus was saying. "Now? At this hour? And in my least presentable nightshirt? Surely, you and your noble companions will be disgraced to be seen in such company. There must be some mistake."

Even with his head down and cradled in his arms Tymmon could hear his father's voice and knew that he was still acting. Pretending a friendly invitation to the intruders to share his amusement at the mistake someone had obviously made, or perhaps at the trick that was being played on some unsuspecting party.

"Good sirs, only stop and consider what you are doing. I am the court jester, gentlemen. Not a priest or surgeon whose services might indeed be needed at midnight in the event of illness or injury. But who could possibly require the presence of a fool at midnight—and in his nightshirt? By whose orders have you come for me, pray tell? Surely not by order of the king!"

"No, not on the old king's orders." Another was speaking now, a younger, higher voice than that of the black-helmeted leader. "But by command of—" There was a thud and the voice stopped with a grunt, as if someone had thumped him into silence.

"The boy." The leader's gonglike voice rang out again. "Where is he? Search for him, Nondum. And you, Wilfar. Find him. He must be here somewhere."

There followed the clatter of furniture overturned and cupboards ransacked, but the one large room held few hiding places and the search did not take long. When silence fell, the black-helmeted one spoke again and his voice was threatening.

"All right, fool. Tell us at once. Where is he? Where is the boy?" And when Komus answered, it was in a halting, jerking voice, as if he were being shaken as he spoke.

"I was trying to tell you"—the words came out in strange bursts and pauses—"but your men were making such a great noise dismantling my home that I could not make myself heard. The boy has gone. He has left Austerneve. Gone forth to seek his fortune in foreign lands."

There was a silent pause before Black Helmet answered. "I do not believe you. You are lying. He was seen in the courtyard only a day or so since, and he was not mentioned in the guard's reports on arrivals and departures."

"Aha," Komus said. "But the guards would not have seen him go. As you may know, sir, the guards at the small postern gate often retire to the guardhouse during the late hours of the night. And because he wanted to leave without great notice, not wishing to distress his friends or spend valuable time on lengthy farewells, my son timed his departure for those lonely hours." Komus's voice suddenly grew louder and more distinct. "Indeed, it was on my advice that he timed his departure in such a way. It is better, I advised him, to leave for a new life in a discreet and humble way, and wait until one returns, having found fame and fortune, to pass through the great gate of the city triumphantly, in the fullness of . . ."

There was a thud and a muffled moan, and then the black-snouted one's deep voice saying "Enough, fool. Spare us your gibbering. We have you and we will find the boy soon enough. And if we find you have lied to us—if we find that he is still here in the castle—that blow will seem to have been no more than the pat of a child."

The shuffle of feet and clanking of swords began again and then died away and a deep empty silence took its place. Only Tymmon remained in the northwest tower, lying facedown on the high ledge with his head wrapped in his trembling arms.

TWO

T ime passed unnoted and uncounted—perhaps only a few endless minutes, but possibly much longer, before Tymmon so much as lifted his head. Lying stiff and still against the window bars, his bones and muscles no longer seemed to be under his control. Only his mind was in working order, or at least certainly in motion, racing frantically in all directions, returning again and again to the scene in the flame-lit room, with his father, barefoot and tousled, surrounded by the five armored men. Who were they? Where had they taken him? And why?

Why Komus? Why would armed men come for a harmless jester, as if he had done murder or committed treachery against his liege lord and country. And then there was the other *why* that kept returning even more insistently—why had the armed men wanted him, too? Wanted Tymmon, son of Komus, who was certainly blameless and not even grown to full manhood.

And then back to the scene in the torchlit room and Komus, playing the fool as always, chattering away to the huge armored men as if they had come on a friendly visit. Chattering about how they were making a mistake, which obviously wasn't true, and how Tymmon had left Austerneve to seek his fortune, which wasn't true either.

But then Tymmon suddenly realized that there had been a purpose behind that bit of chatter. Clearly Komus had said what he did in order to make the intruders think it was useless to search further for Tymmon. And then, at last, another bit of meaning behind Komus's babbling became apparent. The story about how Tymmon had left the castle *by the postern gate in the early hours of the morning.*

Remembering how Komus had raised his voice to almost a shout as he spoke those particular words, it suddenly became quite clear. Komus had been speaking to him, giving him advice about what to do, and how and when. Which meant, of course, that he had known about the window ledge and Tymmon's use of it. And having guessed that he was there, was warning him to leave Austerneve.

But how could he leave? Where would he go? Although Tymmon had often planned to leave the castle and go forth to seek a new life for himself, he had seen himself going as a strong young man, equipped with horse and armor, and all the other necessities for travel in the great outside world.

But to go now? Into the forests inhabited by wild animals and bands of cutthroat robbers and other dangers too horrible to name? Tales told by Mistress Mim, his old nurse, raced through his mind. Tales of horrible creatures, hideous demons, small but deadly imps, and great fire-breathing monsters. Things that, beyond the protecting walls of church and castle, forever haunted the dark mysteries of night. Shuddering, he crossed himself several times over, and then shook his head and went on shaking it. No. No, it was impossible for him to go out now into that haunted darkness.

But to stay? Where could he hide in Austerneve and stay hidden perhaps for many days or weeks? He thought of the hiding places that he and Lonfar had discovered within the castle grounds. Cubbyholes in crooked corners of stables and granaries, nooks and crannies in attics and cellars.

He could indeed hide in such a place. And at one time he could have counted on Lonfar to help him, bringing him food and warning him of impending danger. But not anymore. He could no longer count on Lonfar for anything, and without a source of food he could not stay hidden for long. And when he came out to seek it he would be caught, and then . . . What was it Black Helmet had said he would do to Komus if he found that he was lying about Tymmon's whereabouts? No. He must go. For Komus's sake, as much as for his own.

Suddenly, without even arriving at a decision to do so, he found himself sliding over the edge of the window ledge and making his way slowly down to the floor.

The descent was not easy, complicated by trembling fingers and quivering knees, and once he missed a foothold and almost fell. But at last he reached the floor and groped his way to the hearth, stubbing his toes against overturned chairs and tripping over other fallen and scattered objects. When he reached the fireplace he took a candle from the mantel, held its wick to the embers, and when it finally flamed, turned to see a scene of ruin and destruction.

In the dim light of the candle the entire room was a confused chaos. Open trunks spilled their contents upon the floor, overturned cupboards lay in the midst of broken crockery and spilled flagons. Even the wine barrel had been upended, so that much of the floor was covered by a dark red flood.

Somehow it was the wine barrel that was the most frightening—the shallow red sea more heart-stopping than all the rest of the destruction. For a moment Tymmon didn't know why, but then he understood. The trunks and cupboards might only have been raided in the search for Tymmon, but the intruders could not have expected to find a boy in a barrel of wine. So the spilling of the wine had been an act of needless violence, without cause or reason. Which made all of it, the armed men, the search, and the taking of Komus, seem an act of meaningless cruelty. Not a joke or a mistake or a misunderstanding, but something brutal and savage beyond reason or purpose.

It was an understanding that shook Tymmon like a deep chill and made his hands tremble so that it was hard for him even to settle the candle into a holder and place it on the mantel. He whispered a prayer to the Blessed Mother and then forced himself to stop and gather his wits and prepare to follow his father's advice—to leave Austerneve Castle before the light of morning.

He dressed hastily, pulling on breeches, boots, doublet, jerkin, and his warm winter cloak. A sheet of heavy linen spilling out of an overturned trunk caught his eye and he spread it out on his bed and then began to search through the debris for provisions for his journey. Wading through the wine he located a loaf of bread, a small chunk of salted beef, and a round of cheese.

What else? It was of the greatest importance that he choose wisely. He must not carry so much that he would be unable to move swiftly, and yet he must not forget those things that would be necessary to survival alone in the fields and forests.

Choose wisely. But how, when his mind jittered and jumped with fear and continually interrupted his attempts to think clearly by imagining sounds—the scuff of heavy footsteps on the stairs and the clink and rattle of armor.

But even in his haste and fear he managed to remember a tinderbox, a knife, and a small ax. A few more articles of clothing, chosen almost at random, a blanket, a length of rope—all good useful choices.

Remembering his rosary, a gift from his old nurse, he was lifting it down from a peg above his bed, when his fingers touched another object that hung there. His old flute. And although he had not played in many months, his fingers curled longingly around the familiar shape and held on until it, too, was added to the pack. Then he tied the ends of the sheet together with a stout cord and slung it over his back.

At the door he turned and looked back. The candle

was still burning on the mantel. He was on his way back to blow it out when something round and hard rolled beneath his foot, and looking down, he saw that it was a bell. One of three bells attached to the three horns that adorned the cap of a court jester. And without plan or purpose he picked up the belled cap and shoved it, too, into his pack. Then he snuffed out the candle and left the room that had been his home since before his earliest memory, and started down the twisting staircase into a darkness that seemed deeper than any he had ever known.

Groping his way on the worn stones of the tower staircase, he came at last to ground level, and the broad oaken door that gave onto the alley. It was unbarred. Of course, it must have been or the armed men could not have entered. But how had it come to be so? Komus always slid the heavy bolts home before darkness fell. Could he have forgotten on this one fateful night?

But the mystery was soon solved when, as Tymmon pushed against the door, it gave way, but not by swinging outward. Instead it quivered and then fell out into the alley with a thunderous crash. The intruders had gained entry by removing it from its hinges. While the shattering din still echoed back from the castle's stone walls, Tymmon, his heart thudding in his throat, dashed out the door and away.

Running almost blindly in the near darkness and burdened by his heavy bundle, Tymmon staggered down the alley between workshops and stables, turned the corner at the northern tower, and went on running. Only his familiarity with this passageway, where he had played since earliest childhood, and where every cobblestone was known to him, made it possible for him to keep from falling or dashing headlong into walls or doorposts.

Nearing the church, he remembered a crevice behind a flying buttress and darted into it. He crouched low, listening. Had the intruders heard the crash of the falling door? Minutes passed as he huddled in the hiding place, straining his ears for the sound of approaching footsteps over the thunder of his own heart.

"Go," an inner voice seemed to be telling him. "Go forward. There is no time to waste. Go now."

But his legs refused to obey him, and precious moments passed. Peering out from his hiding place, he suddenly realized that what had seemed only a dark tunnel a few minutes before was now taking on form and substance. Doorways appeared out of the shadows; a bench took shape, and above it a high window. Dawn was approaching. Tymmon glanced upward toward the sky—and suddenly dropped to his knees, cowering in terror.

Lit by the dim light of early day, a face was peering down at him from directly above his head. A terrible face with bulging eyes, a grinning mouth from which protruded a lolling tongue, and ears like small twisted wings. Tymmon had sprung up and begun to run before he suddenly knew what it was that he had seen.

It was only a gargoyle. Only one of the stone monsters that served as drainpipes, funneling water out and away from the church's walls. He had seen the grotesque grinning faces a thousand times—but not in this strange half-light and on so terrible a night.

His pace slowed, but now that he had been jarred loose

from his hiding place he continued on, crossing the church's dooryard and then, by a narrow passageway, on to the edge of the inner courtyard. There he paused again, overtaken once more by panic.

Until now he had been in narrow alleys between the walls of stables and storehouses, but now it was necessary to cross an open space, a small courtyard bordered by wings of the palace, elegant buildings used to house King Austern's guests. And it was now the hour that early-rising servants might well be up and about, fetching water from the well, or sweeping the steps and entryways. Crossing the courtyard would be dangerous, but every moment that he paused would make it even more so. Biting his lip to keep his teeth from chattering, Tymmon went out into the square.

He forced himself to walk, for a running figure would be more apt to arouse interest and suspicion. Bowing his back under the burden of his bundle, he tried to look like a peasant delivering fresh produce—although today was not market day and country folk were not normally allowed in this particular courtyard on any day of the week. But he went on slowly, although at every step the imagined sound of a voice that would command him to stop became louder and clearer in his mind's ear. So loud and clear that when he finally reached the other side, he stopped for a moment in confusion, uncertain what to do next.

On his right now was the fosse, the narrow inner moat that surrounded the castle keep, and to his left, a warehouse and granary. And just beyond the granary was the passageway that led steeply down a cobblestoned ramp to the postern gate. Tymmon ran again now, but softly, try-ing to make no sound. Everything depended on whether the watchmen were awake or asleep, and if he could pass them and open the small but heavy gate without being seen.

A few yards from the guardhouse he slowed again to a walk and then went forward on tiptoe, clenching his teeth against the fearful ragged sound of his own breathing. He drew even with the guardhouse wall and crept on, afraid even to turn his head to look over his shoulder to where the guards would be sleeping—or watching him with an-gry suspicion. But when he was almost past and no one had called to him to stop, he glanced over his shoulder, and there they were, just as Komus had said they would be, sprawled forward across the stone table. As he watched, one of them, old Topad it was, snorted and stirred in his sleep, lifted his head slightly, turned it to face directly toward Tymmon—and went on sleeping.

Two heavy crossbars held the gate, and he was forced to put down his bundle and use all his strength to lift them one by one and slide them back. At his push the gate swung heavily with a muted groan, and he darted out. It wasn't until he had pushed it back into place and started down the path that he remembered his precious bundle. For a moment he wavered, taking two steps for-ward and two back. But surely no fate could be worse than to be a fugitive trying to live off the land—with nothing but empty hands.

Running back frantically, he pulled the gate open a tiny crack and peeked through, to see both of the watchmen now on their feet and staring—but not at him. Standing in the doorway of the guardhouse the two old men were looking up the ramp in the direction from which Tymmon had come. And from beyond them something that had not yet come into Tymmon's range of vision was approaching, clanking and thudding as it came.

He seized his bundle and shoved the gate to. For a moment he leaned against it, gasping with fear. The pathway that led down from the postern gate was long and narrow and zigzagged steeply down the face of the cliff on which Austerneve Castle was built. As it twisted and turned it passed again and again under the turrets and ramparts from which boiling oil had once been poured down upon would-be invaders. And it also passed, again and again, in full view of anyone standing outside the postern entry.

If they opened the gate and came out he was doomed— or would have been if this pathway down to the village of Qweasle had not been, for many years, a favorite playground for Tymmon and Lonfar. Only a few yards away a stunted, wind-twisted tree grew up out of the cliff face just below the surface of the path. Below the leaning tree the cliff fell away sharply, a sheer drop to the next crossing of the path almost fifty feet below. But if one was agile and daring enough one could drop down onto the thick trunk and then swing beneath it into a shallow depression beneath a network of exposed roots.

Tymmon was crouching in the Troll's Lair, as he and Lonfar had named the shallow cave, when the two guards, and others—unseen, but surely the same men who had taken Komus—came through the gate and stood almost directly above him. There was the squeak and clank of armor, the thud of heavy footsteps, and the mutter of muffled voices. And then the voice of Black Helmet, hollow and gonglike, rang out clearly.

"Then tell me, old man. If, as you say, no one has passed through this gate since yesterday, why were the bars not in place? Is it not part of your duty to see that the bars are set at nightfall and remain so until dawn?"

Another familiar voice, that of old Topad, spoke then. "It is indeed, good sir. But the Qweasle stonemasons are expected soon, and I had just opened the bars in preparation for their early arrival when your lordships came upon us. But no one has yet passed through the gate this morning. If your lordships are looking for someone in particular, we will be glad to watch for such a person and send him to your lordships when he arrives."

"Very good." A new voice was speaking now, high-pitched and youthful. "You should be on the lookout for . . ."

But at that point Black Helmet spoke again, his voice blurring into a meaningless roar. A long pause followed and then the sound of heavy clanking footsteps began again and gradually faded into nothing. When the sound had completely died away, Swiffer, the other watchman, spoke accusingly.

"You lied about the bars, Topad."

"Yes, I lied, Swiffer. To protect your worthless hide. Was it not your turn to bar the gate last night?"

"It was. And I did. I particularly remember the barring last night because it was then that I caught my third finger behind the bar and mashed it badly. See how bruised it is. Do you not remember how I remarked about it?"

Old Topad laughed. *"Remarked,* indeed. *Cursed* might better describe your comments, as I recall. But that was two days ago. Your mind is playing tricks on you again."

"Or yours on you. I am certain 'twas but last night."

For a moment the watchmen's voices gave way to silence, and then Swiffer spoke again. "Seems strange," he said.

"What seems strange to you now, old friend?"

"That our recent visitors hid their faces behind lowered visors, although they were not under attack or even the threat of it."

"That is so. And that their leader seemed not to want us to know the object of their search. Did you notice how he stopped the one who would have told us?"

"So he did."

There was another pause, and then Topad said, "Ah, well, it is not for the likes of us to try to understand the behavior of noble men-at-arms."

Then the gate's hinges groaned again and silence fell. And in the small cave beneath the bent tree Tymmon crouched low over his bundle and prayed for the strength and courage to continue his journey.

THREE

I t could not have been long that Tymmon waited in the temporary safety of the tiny cave before he made ready to continue his journey. Only long enough for his heartbeat to slow slightly and for his shaking hands to become steady enough to lift his bundle and tie it back across his shoulders. But by then it was already too late.

He was just beginning the dangerous climb up to the pathway when he stopped suddenly and scrambled back into the hollow behind the hanging roots. The sound of voices was drifting up the steep hillside from somewhere far below.

Safely back in his hiding place, he inched forward and peered down. On a stretch of path several turnings below the cave a half dozen workmen were trudging upward, laden with the heavy tools of their trade. Clearly there had been some truth in Topad's excuse for the unbarred postern gate. The stonemasons of Qweasle were indeed arriving early for work in the castle grounds.

The workmen, dressed in homespun smocks and tattered leggings, wound their way slowly up the zigzag path, chatting and laughing as they came. The sound grew louder as they crossed above Tymmon's hiding place and then faded as they reached the gateway and rang the bell for entrance.

But the stonemasons' voices had scarcely died away when others took their place and three old women, village seamstresses on their way to work in the castle's sewing rooms, began the long climb. They were moving even more slowly, and before they finally reached their destination, the sun was well up and, at the foot of Austerneve Tor, the village of Qweasle was up and stirring.

There was little chance now that Tymmon could make his way through the scattering of shops and homes, past the central square with its fountain where there was a constant throng of water carriers and washerwomen, and across the church courtyard with its usual gatherings of old men, without being seen by someone he knew.

If Black Helmet and his men had already visited the village offering rewards for his capture he would possibly be stopped and held prisoner. And even if the villagers let him pass he could not stop their tongues from wagging. When Komus's captors did arrive they would soon learn, not only that Tymmon, son of Komus the jester, had passed that way, but also exactly when. And then Black Helmet would punish Komus for lying about when his son had left Austerneve.

They would punish Komus. How would they punish him? Horrible possibilities pushed their way into Tymmon's mind. He had himself witnessed punishments meted out to commoners by angry nobles. Even under the rule of kindly old King Austern there had been public beatings, imprisonment in tiny cages, and once, long ago, a beheading. And he had heard of even more terrible tortures in other kingdoms.

No, he could *not* be seen today in Qweasle. It was a risk that, for Komus's sake, could not be taken. And there was only one way to avoid it. Arranging his lumpy bundle into a makeshift pillow, Tymmon prepared to stay where he was, in the cold, damp hollow beneath the twisted tree, until the day ended and darkness returned.

The weather continued cold and gray, and the wind, sweeping up the face of the cliff, curled in and out of the shallow cave like a current of icy water. Wrapped in his long cape and blanket, Tymmon tried to still his chattering teeth and keep his mind on other things.

He thought first and longest about what had happened and what it could all mean. There were so many unanswered questions: Who was the man in the helmet that looked like the grotesque face of some shiny black beast? And who had sent him? And why?

Of one thing he was certain. Black Helmet and his men, although they wore the armor and carried the arms of noblemen, were not members of King Austern's court. In a castle community as small as Austerneve, every permanent resident knew every other at least by sight. And Tymmon, to whom men-at-arms were objects of passionate interest, knew the armor and bearings of all of Austerneve's noble knights. He would quickly recognize, for instance, Lonfar's father, Sir Hildar, by the azure orle and eagle fess point emblazoned on his shield and breastplate. And even if his armorial bearings were not visible, Tymmon would certainly recognize him by his old flat-topped helmet.

The noble knight, Sir Hildar. Tymmon's thoughts were tinged with bitterness as his mind drifted back to Lonfar, his onetime friend. And to the days when he and Lonfar had first studied together under Komus's tutelage. When they had daily helped each other to learn, not only reading and writing, but also all the ancient lore that Lonfar, as a future knight, was expected to master.

Actually, it had been Tymmon who had done most of the helping since it was he, the son of a lowly court jester, who had been much quicker to memorize every fess and bar and dexter, every lion guardant and dragon rampant, on the armorial bearings of scores of noble families. Lonfar had often said that it was a shame that, because of his lowly birth, Tymmon could not hope to someday be a noble knight. Sometimes it had been said in a kindly and regretful way. But at other times, when Tymmon had been slow to do his bidding, it was said sharply, as a means of reminding Tymmon of his duty to be humble and obedient when in noble company.

Tymmon sighed, and shivered, and brought his thoughts back to the problems at hand. To the cold, damp cave, and to the question of the armed men. That their armor was not familiar was most strange. And stranger still, he could not remember seeing any heraldic markings on their breastplates. Of course the light had been dim and flickering, and he had been looking down from high above, but still he would surely have noted such bearings had they been visible. It was possible, of course, for men-at-arms to cover their breastplates with unmarked tunics in order to keep their identity secret.

For a while Tymmon toyed with the idea that the intruders might have been brigands, one of the bands of cutthroat highwaymen who lived in forests and other deserted places and came out to rob and murder highborn travelers and lowly country folk alike.

The kingdom of Austerneve had good reason to fear such outlaws, since it was such a band that, three years before, had kidnapped and killed Prince Mindor, King Austern's only son and heir. That terrible day would never fade from Tymmon's memory. He and Lonfar had been playing in the central courtyard near the great gate when a messenger arrived with the news that plunged the whole kingdom into mourning.

The people had mourned not only for the sorrow of their beloved old king, but for themselves as well. For a people ruled by an aging king whose only heir was a little granddaughter, who was then a child scarcely out of infancy.

Tymmon had grieved in particular for poor little Princess Amica, a slight, pale child whom he had often seen at play in the inner courtyard. She seemed to him a lonely child, and knowing that she, like Tymmon himself, had been motherless since infancy, he had always felt for her a special sympathy. And with her father's death she had become a royal orphan. It had seemed strange and terrible to Tymmon that God could have allowed such sorrow to come to a child of such noble birth. And it seemed even more tragic that her father had died at the hands of a scurvy band of brigands, instead of in glorious battle as would seem right and proper for a royal personage such as Prince Mindor of Austerneve.

Brigands had indeed been a terrible scourge in all of the North Countries. But on further thought it seemed unlikely to Tymmon that the five intruders had been brigands, since their arms and armor had been that of noblemen and the brigand bands were said to be made up of commoners—renegade peasants and deserters from the ranks of ordinary foot soldiers.

The five knights could, of course, have been recent arrivals or even simply visitors to Austerneve. Noble visitors to the castle came and went constantly, and many of them were unfamiliar to Tymmon. But that possibility made the taking of Komus even more senseless. Why would some outsider, someone who knew little of Austerneve and its people, capture and carry away a court jester—a person of no rank or importance although a great favorite of the old king? That was a question that returned again and again. Why would anyone abduct a simple court jester? Why Komus? And then—why my father?

"My father," Tymmon whispered, and the words caught in his throat, and ached there with a raw, throbbing pain. He swallowed hard and shook his head angrily, but the ache remained. And when he probed the pain, saying "my father" again and then again, it only grew stronger.

"My father," he said aloud, and somehow the saying was not in his present, almost manly voice, but in the high-pitched tones of a child. High-pitched, and trembling with emotions that were also not of the present, but filled instead with old, almost forgotten feelings of unquestioning love, and admiration—and pride.

He had been proud of Komus then—back then as a child of six or seven years. Proud of the way Komus the jester was known and greeted by everyone in the castle and village as well. Proud that Komus could read and write, as few in Austerneve could, and that he could make music on lyre and rebec and flute that set people dancing or brought tears to their eyes. But that had been years ago, and since that time Tymmon's thoughts and feelings concerning the court jester of Austerneve had undergone many changes.

But other, sharper, pains finally demanded his attention, bringing him back to the tiny cramped hollow in which he lay. He was, he began to realize, not only cold and stiff but very hungry as well. Loosening the knots that held his pack, he brought out the cheese and bread and broke off small pieces, reminding himself to eat sparingly as it might be long before he was able to find other food. But the bread was dry and rough, and without water or wine to wash it down he found it hard to swallow even that small allowance.

The hours passed at a slow, painful crawl. The wind remained strong and cold, and all that day there was no sunlight to turn Austerneve Tor into a gigantic sundial, as it did in better weather when the castle's shadow reached out across the village of Qweasle as the afternoon wore on.

Now and then Tymmon slept briefly, only to awake in

horror from threatening dreams. Cold and thirst and the ache of cramped muscles became more and more unbearable and at last turned into a kind of rage that made him twist and turn and flail about inside his narrow prison, kicking the confining walls or pounding them with his fists.

Toward sundown he slept again and dreamt once more, but this time not of helpless horror but of brave deeds and enemies vanquished. In this dream he was once more on the high ledge in the tower room and Black Helmet and his men were again breaking down the door. But this time when Komus stepped out from behind the bed curtains he, too, was wearing the armor of a knight and wielding a huge shining sword. And Tymmon, leaping down from the ledge with fierce delight, was also in armor. And together they attacked the intruders, beating them back through the doorway and down the stairs.

To awake cold and stiff, alone and frightened, after so glorious a dream was torture and treachery and torment, and Tymmon's anger grew stronger than ever. He raged at Black Helmet and his men, who had driven him out of his home into the cold and dangerous world, and even at King Austern, who must have allowed such evil men to come as guests to Austerneve.

But deep down, and bitterer for being shameful and unnatural, Tymmon's anger turned toward Komus himself. Toward Komus, who had been weak and helpless before the invaders of his home, and who had tried, pitiably, to use wit and humor as weapons against five armed knights.

"You could have had real weapons," he found himself

whispering. "You could have defended yourself in honor-able combat if only you had not . . ." He paused and then, pounding his fist against the damp earth in frustra-tion, he asked again, as he had asked so many times with-out answer or explanation, "Why? Why? Why?"

So Tymmon, tormented by cold and thirst and hunger, tortured himself further by harsh and bitter thoughts un-til at last a procession of castle laborers returning to their homes in the village foretold the end of the day. The sun sank behind the far hills, and darkness crept across the valley. In Qweasle the old men left the square, and even the fountain courtyard was deserted. And stiff and sore, Tymmon climbed up the network of roots, worked his way up the sloping tree trunk, and scrambled onto the pathway below the postern gate.

It was good to stand erect again and to move freely, even though he moved through near darkness and into the unknown. For a while he strode bravely, telling him-self that he was off and away on a grand adventure, a quest for some great and glorious destiny. But on the last length of the pathway his step slowed, and when he reached the edge of the dark village, it became little more than a crawl.

He would have to make his way through Qweasle si-lently and with extreme caution. Although the villagers usually retired early, there was still the possibility of a chance meeting with some ale drinker returning to his cottage after a visit to the barroom of the inn. Or some lovesick young man might yet be afoot after calling at the home of his beloved. And there was always the danger of a wakeful watchdog that might arouse the village with his barking.

Moving silently through the deepest shadows, he passed the blacksmith's shop and the inn safely, but he was just entering the central square when there was a sound of pattering feet and the squeak of a bucket handle. Hastily, Tymmon drew back into the shadows and watched as someone approached the fountain. Out in the center of the courtyard the darkness was less complete and it was soon possible to make out the figure of a small villager. A boy of no more than nine or ten years, who was whistling bravely but not too confidently through his teeth and glancing anxiously in all directions as he drew up water to fill his pail.

Tymmon grinned. Then without stopping to think of possible consequences, he pulled the hood of his cape down over his face, and uttering a hair-raising moan he glided out into the square. The results were exactly what he expected, or should have if he had stopped to think. The little boy threw his pail in the air, screeched in terror, and took off running like a frightened hare. And belatedly realizing the stupidity of what he had done, Tymmon ran too, across the square and toward the alley that led to the storage yard behind the marketplace.

In a moment every dog in Qweasle was barking and the village was full of half-dressed men, waving staffs or pitchforks and shouting questions as they ran wildly in all directions.

Tymmon had not yet reached the alley when he was suddenly confronted by two men armed with heavy clubs.

Snatching up a length of firewood from a doorway, he waved it over his head and ran to meet them.

"What happened?" he shouted. "Which way did they go?" And when the men ran on he pretended to follow until the next corner, when he doubled back toward the marketplace. He passed several other searchers in the same fashion and at last gained the alley, dashed through the storage yard and out into the empty meadow.

He went on running until the sounds of shouting and barking were far away in the distance, and even then he staggered on, across rock-strewn, uneven ground, his heavy pack pounding against his back, its rough rope bindings digging into his shoulders. He crossed a hayfield, an open meadow, and went on until, reeling from exhaustion, he reached the shelter of a thick stand of trees and sank to the ground.

Sprawled face downward in the deep grass he gasped for breath, his throat burning and his lungs on fire. The pain brought anger. Anger at himself for doing such a foolish, dangerous thing, and then, as so often happened, at Komus.

That was a Komus trick, he told himself. If he had been caught and delivered up to Black Helmet, it would have been Komus's fault. Komus's fault because—well, because one could not live all one's life with a joker and clown without becoming, to some extent, a joker oneself. So it was obviously his father's example that had made him do what he did. Had made him risk everything to play the role of a phantom of the night, in order to frighten a poor little village boy within an inch of his life.

Tymmon found himself grinning again. It had been—

amusing. And the way his other ruse had worked, the way he had saved himself by pretending to be one of the would-be rescuers. He actually found himself chuckling for a brief moment before he slowly became aware of his surroundings. Became aware of a dank woodsy chill and of the rustling darkness all around him. And it came to him suddenly in a great wave of terror that he was alone at nightfall—in the Sombrous Forest.

Inching backward until he encountered the trunk of a large tree, Tymmon curled himself up against it like a frightened hedgehog and buried his head in his arms.

FOUR

Night settled over the Sombrous, the deepest, darkest, and most feared forest in all of the North Countries. The stories of the forest's terrors had been a part of Tymmon's childhood, growing up as he had in Castle Austern, where it could be seen from the highest battlements—a dark green ocean stretching away to the farthest horizons.

According to Mistress Mim no man in his right mind entered the forest at night. And many of his other friends and acquaintances had said the same. Some said that not even the fierce and fearless brigand bands, who often roamed the forest during the day, would allow themselves to be caught within its endless green maze after nightfall.

"Shun the Sombrous when the sun has set," was a saying that Tymmon had known and heeded for years. He would not, in fact, have entered its shadowed pathways, either by day or night, if he had been given a choice. But one has little choice when pursued by an angry mob.

Actually he had been in the forest once before—but not alone and in broad daylight. That had been some years earlier, when he and Lonfar had gone to Qweasle to play with the village boys. Although both Tymmon and Lonfar had often given their word never to venture into the forest, on this particular day they had allowed their village friends to persuade them to forget their promises.

"We'll go only as far as the river," the boys had said. " 'Tis not dangerous now at midday, and the Sombrous River is a thing to see. Unless you are afraid."

So of course they had no choice but to go, and the forest and river had indeed been things to see and remember. The forest was beautiful, Tymmon remembered—and awful. He could still recall how the tall trees marched away in every direction, like colonnades of noble pillars in some immense cathedral. A cathedral roofed by endlessly overlapping green canopies, through which rays of spangled sunlight slanted downward like shining pathways to heaven. He could remember how the rough bark of the surrounding trunks wore, on one side, a green velvet mantle of mosses, and how beds of small, soft-hued flowers made bright carpets on the damp forest floor.

But there were other memories—of dense clumps of underbrush that rustled threateningly as they passed, and of strange haunting cries, like those of a lost soul that now and then echoed faintly through the still air. But most frightening of all were the endless twistings and turnings, crossings and recrossings of the forest trails. He could still picture quite clearly in his mind's eye how the pathways, like long green tunnels each looking exactly like the last, led off in every direction—tempting the intruder to follow —into an endless forest maze from which there would be no rescue or return.

Many times that day Tymmon's heart had swollen with a terrible anxiety, the deep instinctive fear of being hopelessly and endlessly lost. But the village boys had known which trails to follow, and after a time they had come out upon the banks of a wide river and eventually returned safely to the open farmland. But that daring forest visit had been in the company of others and in daylight. And now it was night, a night as deep as death and seemingly as endless.

Curled up in a ball against the tree trunk, Tymmon slept but little, tortured by cold and thirst and fear. As the hours crept by, thirst became the greatest torment. He had not drunk since the night before and now his throat was parched and dry and his tongue felt swollen. When he slept he dreamt of water, and when he awakened his mind returned again and again to the river he had visited on that long-ago expedition.

But to try to find the river at night and alone would surely be hopeless, and terribly dangerous as well. Even so, at one point the torment of his thirst became so unbearable that he made up his mind to go in search of water.

He would get to his feet, he decided, and feel his way through the night until he found the river. But he had gone no more than a few steps before the solid unbroken darkness and the faint mysterious sounds, like that of stealthy motion, overcame his resolve, and he found himself again crouched against the tree trunk, trembling with fear.

He would wait until the first light of dawn, he told himself, and then he would go to the river. But when morning came the need for water was no longer his greatest problem. Sometime in the small hours of the morning it had begun to rain, and there was water all around him. Now his greatest need was for warmth and shelter.

Having drunk from one of the small pools that had sprung up in the deeper hollows of the forest floor, and eaten a few mouthfuls of his rapidly dwindling supply of food, Tymmon retied his bundle, got to his feet, and started down the nearest green tunnel—but to where?

He could go on, and if he were fortunate he might eventually find the river. He would then have plenty of water—but what of food, and shelter from the rain and cold? And what if he could not find his way out? And what if, in his lost and lonely wanderings, he came upon a huge black bear or a pack of gray wolves? Or—he could hardly bear to think of it—what if he found himself in a grove of dead trees and looking up, saw drifting down upon him an evil black shadow and heard the shrill screech of a harpy?

Harpies had been occasional haunters of Tymmon's most terrible nightmares for many years. He had always believed completely in their existence, although Komus said he doubted their reality since he had never seen one, nor met anyone who had. But that proved nothing, since Komus seemed to believe in very little, not even in such obvious realities as evil spirits, guardian angels, and the ability of witches to curse herds of milk cows into barren uselessness. And if Komus had not met anyone who had seen a harpy it only meant, perhaps, that those who actually saw one did not live to tell of it. And while it might be true that people who had actually seen a harpy were not numerous, Tymmon knew a great many people, including Mistress Mim, who knew all about them and believed in them completely.

A harpy, according to his old nurse, was a horrible creature, disgustingly filthy and terrible to look upon. In shape they were half bird and half woman, winged and feathered, with huge clawlike feet whose talons were sharper than any razor. Their faces were those of lovely young maidens except for their wild, cruel eyes and the blood that continually smeared their mouths and dripped from their small, sharp teeth. They lived deep in the forest in groves of dead trees, for their evil was so poisonous that the very trees where they nested soon withered and died.

Everyone who spoke of harpies described them so, and such tales were much on Tymmon's mind as he left his resting place at the edge of the forest. He had gone only a few yards down the first faint trail when he came upon the dry, leafless skeleton of a long-dead tree. Turning, he fled in panic back to the edge of the clearing.

Wet, cold, terribly tired from a lack of rest and sleep, and more miserable than he had ever been before or dreamed of being, Tymmon crouched again in the same spot where he had spent the night, and tried to think and plan.

To go out again into the open farmlands of the valley would put him in almost certain danger from Black Helmet and his men. But the dangers of the forest, no matter how unseen and uncertain, seemed at the moment more terrible. At last he rose, and pulling the sodden hood of his cape close around his face, he ventured out across the open fields in a southerly direction, into the valley but away from Qweasle and Austerneve Tor.

The day continued dark and damp with a thin, steady drizzle of rain, and Tymmon's long cape and even the bundle on his back soon became heavy with water. Crossing the open meadow, he slogged through marshy places that smeared his shoes and gaiters with thick mud. At the edge of a wheat field he came upon a large dirty gray mound, the remains of an old haystack. There, after digging below its wet and moldering exterior, he was able to make himself a cave that was cold and musty but comparatively dry. Unlashing his bundle and finding that his blanket was somewhat drier than his sodden cloak, he wrapped himself in it and quickly fell asleep.

On waking some hours later, he found that the rain had stopped and a weak sun was waning and he would have to hurry on, to put as much distance as possible between himself and Austerneve before nightfall. After crossing several more fields planted to rye and flax he came at last to a road. At the moment it was deserted—a wide, bare ribbon of muddy earth stretching out to the horizon. He would, he decided, follow the road, as it would undoubtedly lead to other villages or farms where he might find food and shelter, perhaps in exchange for labor.

He started off along the roadway, but he had not gone far when the jingle of harness and the thud of hooves warned him that horsemen were approaching. Scurrying to hide behind a clump of brambles that grew beside the road, he crouched low as a party of horsemen approached from the north and rode by at a smart trot.

There were nine or ten riders in all. Apparently three or four knights accompanied by their squires, pages, and other attendants. They were not Austerneve men-at-arms, nor did any of them wear a snouted helmet of black metal, of that much he was certain. However, squinting through the tangle of brambles, he was not able to see clearly enough to make out such details as the devices on their shields and breastplates. But they had come from the north, where they might well have met and spoken with Black Helmet and his followers. So Tymmon remained hidden and waited until the whole troop had disappeared far down the road before he ventured out and continued on his journey.

Tired and hungry, wet and smeared with mud, he trudged on and on, placing one cold, numb foot ahead of the other in weary desperation. Beside the road, culti-vated fields alternated with rough untilled pasture land, but there was no sign of farm or village.

It was some hours later, and to the west over the now distant forest the sky was turning to shades of orange and red, before he saw the first sign of human habitation, a column of smoke twisting up into the sunset sky. Turning in that direction, Tymmon was soon able to see the thatched roofs of a cluster of farm buildings. It seemed to be a well-kept and prosperous farm. Surely at such a place there would be some task that a willing worker might do in exchange for food and shelter.

At first the farmyard seemed deserted, but as Tymmon drew nearer he noticed someone working in a kitchen garden behind the cottage. A sturdy, broad-backed woman, dressed in gray homespun, her head covered by veil and wimple, continued to swing her short-handled garden hoe as Tymmon made his way, hopefully, toward her. Hopefully, because a woman—perhaps a mother— surely would be more compassionate toward a homeless wanderer, a poor, pitiful, starving lad who . . .

But there was also a dog. An angry one, by the sound of it, and as Tymmon cleared the corner of the farmhouse he saw it, chained to a post in the dooryard. A short, squat creature, it raved and slobbered as it strained against its collar in its eagerness to attack. Tymmon stopped, hoping desperately that the chain would hold and that the woman would notice and quiet her watchdog. But she only shouted something and went on hoeing, and then a man appeared who was almost as threatening as the dog.

Coming out from behind a stable, so bearded and bushy-haired as to arouse fearful thoughts of monsters and werewolves, the man strode toward the chained animal shaking a heavy spade over his head.

"Quiet, Wolf! Hush, you demented creature. Quiet, before I give you something to howl about." The dog stopped barking and cowered in the dirt, and the man changed directions.

"You there," he shouted. "Who are you? What are you doing on my land?"

Tymmon's knees threatened to betray him and send him, like the dog, cowering to the earth. But he managed to stand his ground, and when the farmer came to a stop only a few feet away, he pushed back his hood, held his head erect, and tried to smile.

"Greetings, kind sir," he said. "My name is Tymmon, son of Komus, and I am traveling in search of my fortune. I would only like . . ."

A large hand grasped his shoulder roughly and the farmer's deep-set eyes glared into his. "Komus?" the deep voice said. "That is a good northland name, but you look like no northlander I have seen. A gypsy you are or I mistake myself. And I'll have no gypsies on my land. Now get you out of here before I set Wolf loose on you."

"Wait, Arl." It was the woman from the garden, who was now hurrying toward them. "Wait. Let the boy stay. Go to the dooryard, boy, and wait for us by the well. I must speak with my husband. Go now!"

"What are you saying, woman," the farmer shouted. "The gypsy leaves. I'll have no . . ."

Tymmon had started toward the well when he heard something that made him stop in midstep and strain his ears to listen. The conversation went on, and although he could not make out the whispered words of the woman, he heard clearly enough her husband's answering bellow.

"What horsemen? I saw no horsemen today." And then after a pause in which his wife again whispered urgently, "An escaped fugitive? Three silver pieces? A reward of three silver pieces for a half-grown boy? You are dreaming, woman." There was more whispering and then the man whirled around, bellowing more loudly still. "Boy. Where are you? Come back here, lad."

But Tymmon was already off and running, around the corner of the cottage, across the stableyard, over a rail fence and out across the pasture toward the west. Toward the west, where the Sombrous was now a silhouette of black velvet domes and spires against a bloodred sky.

He reached the edge of the forest at twilight and stumbled in among the first tall trees, shaking with fear and exhaustion. He had been running in panic for what seemed an eternity, running and falling, leaping up to run again, stopping only from time to time to listen desperately for the sound of pursuit—for the shouts of the farmer and the baying of his ferocious dog. But each time the painful rasp of his own breathing drowned out all other sound. And so he had run again and again until at last he reached the forest.

Beneath the light-blocking canopy he moved more slowly, working his way around tree trunks and clumps of yew and elderberry, telling himself the farmer would not follow him here—at least not until daylight. No one would risk the blinding darkness and the demons that haunted . . . A whimper interrupted Tymmon's musings, a pitiful, timorous sound that had somehow arisen from his own throat. Clamping his teeth against another such unmanly utterance, he sank to a crouch and began to creep backwards. He had retreated for several yards before he stopped—overtaken by a sudden promising idea.

A fire. He would build a fire. It was said that a bright blaze would frighten away wild beasts. And perhaps its revealing light might even hold at bay other, more dreadful, things. Or at least make it possible to see what was approaching before its teeth were fastened in his throat.

But it would have to be done quickly before the dim red-tinged twilight died away to complete darkness.

Back among the tall trees he cast about until he found a small clearing, where he quickly collected a large heap of fallen branches. After preparing a pile of leaves and twigs, he opened the tinderbox and began to strike the flint and steel. A spark flew into the waiting tinder and flared into a flame, which he hastily fed with twigs. Next came branches, and soon Tymmon was sitting beside a roaring fire.

Warmth. The first since he had fled Austerneve. In the comforting glow Tymmon found that he was able, at least for brief moments, to forget that outside the range of his firelight the dark forest night was all around him. Taking off his soggy shoes and clammy cloak, he hung them on a drying rack fashioned from a broken branch. Then he opened his pack and arranged its contents, too, around the fire.

His food was almost gone. Having eaten a few crumbs of bread, a sliver of dried meat, and the last of the cheese, he fed the fire once more before he wrapped himself in his blanket and curled up as near to the flames as he dared. He would not sleep, he told himself, and he did not, or at least not deeply nor for long.

Lying motionless, swaddled in his blanket like a moth in a cocoon, he began to make an astonishing discovery. His body and everything connected to it, the pain of hunger and tired, chilled muscles, seemed to have faded away into a dreamlike distance—still there, but without real significance. Much more urgent and important realities seemed to be taking place elsewhere. But in an elsewhere that he could somehow see and experience.

He could see Castle Austerneve with people coming and going, stopping to talk to each other, or hurrying on about their business. He could see himself and Lonfar wading in the fosse as they used to do on hot days, splashing each other and laughing wildly.

And then, in a vision even more clear and distinct—he was home. He was once again in the round room in the northwest tower, with Komus working at his desk, copying a manuscript and looking up, laughing, to say "Tymmon. Listen to this." And then his smile fading and his face, also. But still repeating softly, as if from a far distance, "Listen, Tymmon. Listen."

Tymmon sat up. The fire had burned low, the darkness pressed nearer, and the silence was deep and absolute. But as he threw back his blanket there was a tinkling chime of small bells. The bells of Komus's cap. For a moment of wild joy he thought his vision was true and he was somehow back in the tower, in their old room, and Komus . . . But then he moved his foot and the bell rang again. Reaching out, he found it lying near his feet—the jester's cap that had been the last thing he added to his pack as he began his flight from Austerneve.

The joy fled. Sadly, Tymmon turned the cap in his hand, running his fingers along the three pointed horns and listening to the tinkling of the bells, a sound he could remember hearing from his earliest childhood. A sound that somehow brought back the strange comfort of the dreamlike visions.

Smiling, he put the cap on his head and sat staring into

the fire, now and then shaking his head gently to hear the familiar chiming of the belled cap—and to bring back the peaceful calm.

The dreamy distance had returned and his thoughts were flying far and free, when a small sharp sound, perhaps the click of claws on pebbles, brought him back to reality. To the reality of the forest clearing, the dying fire, and just beyond it, a hideous inhuman face.

FIVE

❧

T he face was grinning, its loose lips stretched wide to reveal sharp white teeth, its long red tongue lolling to one side.

Frozen with fear, Tymmon gasped, "God help me," and sat motionless, waiting for death. Waiting for the cruel grip of sharp fangs. . . .

But then suddenly he knew—and almost laughed out loud. It was only a gargoyle. Once again he had let himself be fooled by a gargoyle. He smiled sheepishly, excusing his foolish reaction by blaming it on the strange trancelike state he had been experiencing. A condition caused no doubt by hunger and exhaustion. But it was still more than a little embarrassing to give oneself up to die because of a harmless stone image of . . .

The bulging eyes blinked, the grin disappeared, and the tongue flapped up to lick the sagging jowls. Not stone.

Not of stone and, he belatedly realized, certainly not where gargoyles were usually to be found—on the eaves of church or castle. But what then? A monster certainly. A monster so ugly that the mere sight of it might well, like the evil Medusa, turn the viewer to stone.

Tymmon's hand crept up to test his cheek for evidence of hardening. Still soft and warm. He swallowed hard. Swallowed again and tried to speak.

"What—what are you? What do you want of me?"

The monster cocked its head, its jagged bat-wing ears flopping. It certainly looked very like a gargoyle. A new thought occurred. Perhaps it was. Perhaps a magical gargoyle conjured into life by some powerful enchantment.

"Are you an enchanted creature?" he asked. "A gargoyle brought to life?"

The creature cocked its head again, to the other side, and then made a short stiff-legged jump in Tymmon's direction. "Troff," it said.

Tymmon shrank back, expecting its next leap to take it over the fire and . . .

"Troff," it said again with what seemed to be a nod.

A living gargoyle. A gargoyle—perhaps called Troff? "Troff?" Tymmon asked, and moving forward immediately as if it had been summoned, it trotted toward him around the fire. It did not stop until it was standing over where Tymmon cowered back on one elbow, whispering frantic Hail Marys and trying to protect his throat with his free hand. With its enormous head only inches from his face, its rank breath hot on his cheeks, it stared down at Tymmon and licked its chops.

Hungry. It was hungry, and its next meal might well be

. . . Groping desperately behind his back, Tymmon grasped the parcel that held the last of his food, a small piece of salt-cured meat. "Here," he said. "Here, gargoyle. Would you like this good beef? Here, take it. It's yours."

The disappearance of the salted meat occurred in an instant, accompanied by a variety of disgusting chomping and slobbering noises. When the last morsel had disappeared, the monster sat down in front of Tymmon and stared at him with eager expectancy, as if waiting for more. And staring back, Tymmon could only think that he himself was being considered as the next course.

But the creature made no immediate move in his direction, and for the first time Tymmon's terror diminished enough to allow him to study it more closely.

Thick-bodied and long-legged, the gargoyle when on all fours would stand somewhat taller than Tymmon's waist. Its face was a ghostly gray that shaded around the eyes and muzzle to almost black, while its body seemed to be closely covered with a short gray-brown fur. The feet were large and rounded like the paws of lions, and the long tail ended, like a lion's, in a short tuft of black hair. Lionlike it was indeed except for its face, which was a thousand times uglier than any lion. Snub-snouted, fisheyed, with great flapping jowls, it had a mouth that became an upside-down U when closed, and when open, a terrifying cavern filled with long white teeth.

Tymmon shuddered and drew away, and the monster closed its mouth, tipped its head to one side, and regarded him more intently.

"Why?" it seemed to be asking.

"Why am I afraid of you?" Tymmon smiled ruefully and

then went on. "I meet a living gargoyle in the middle of the forest on a dark night, and you wonder why I am afraid? It would seem that gargoyles know very little about humankind."

The gargoyle raised its head and, with what almost seemed to be a grin, asked what Tymmon knew about gargoyles.

"Well." Tymmon considered the question. "Not a great deal, I suppose. Just that they are usually carved from stone and extend from the roofs of buildings."

The gargoyle blinked its bulging eyes and twitched its tail and again asked why.

"To serve as water spouts. And some say to frighten away evil spirits. That's why they are all so ug—" Tymmon paused. "So frightening to look upon."

The creature's mouth dropped open into its evil, tongue-lolling grin. Reaching out, it placed one of its great paws firmly on Tymmon's foot, regarded him sternly, and said that, yes, he was frightening—when he wanted to be. But not always. Then it lay down on its belly, and slowly lowered its great head onto its front paws.

Tymmon watched it with unblinking attention while it yawned, snorted, and mumbled, rolled its eyes, and then closed them firmly. It was not until then that Tymmon crept back under his blanket and pulled it up to his nose. Peering out over the top, he watched the sleeping monster intently for a long time—and then intermittently for several shorter periods in between violent struggles to keep his heavy eyelids from falling shut. But he soon lost the battle and fell asleep—and slept more soundly than he had since leaving Austerneve.

Some hours later Tymmon awoke with a frightened start. Something had made an evil sound, a snuffling snort that was clearly that of some inhuman creature. For a moment he cowered under his blanket until, suddenly remembering the events of the night before, he thrust it aside and peered out. The gargoyle was still there, its great gray-brown body sprawled out near the dead ashes of the fire. Tymmon pushed the blanket to one side and leaped to his feet, forgetting that Komus's cap was still on his head. At the ringing of the bells the creature was instantly alert and staring with that eager expectancy that once again made Tymmon uneasy.

"There is no more meat, Troff," he said hastily. "I have nothing more to give you. But I am going to go now to look for food."

The gargoyle jumped up, stretched, and opened its great mouth in a growling yawn and then said something eager and enthusiastic about the possibility of food.

To look for food. But where? It was a question that must be answered quickly since he himself was already dangerously weak and light-headed from hunger. And the gargoyle was obviously also hungry, which might well be even more dangerous. He must find food and very soon. Here in the forest there might be wild game such as deer and rabbits, but to live by hunting required a bow and arrow and the skill to use them. No, it would have to be the highroad and farm and village, no matter what the danger from Black Helmet and his men.

"Troff," Tymmon said, and the gargoyle moved nearer, its ears cocked. "I'm going to have to leave the forest and go to the nearest village and find food, even if I have to beg for it. So I'll be leaving soon."

The ears drooped and Tymmon imagined that the monster looked regretful, but it made no comment and Tymmon moved away to gather up his belongings. A moment later, when he turned back, the grove was empty. "Troff?" he said softly and then louder, "Troff," but there was no response and nothing stirred in the underbrush that surrounded the clearing.

Tymmon sank down against a tree trunk and remained there for some time lost in thought. Where had it gone so suddenly, and what kind of magical creature had it been? Magical surely, since it had the power of speech—or did it? Had he heard the things it said with his ears, or in some other manner? It was a question that, for some reason, had not even occurred to him before. But now, in recollection, it seemed that it had not been through his ears that the gargoyle's thoughts echoed in his mind. It was instead as if its thinking reflected inside his own head, in the manner that still water reflects all that it is near.

But magical or not, what it had surely been was a monstrous creature that came out of the night and slept at his feet like a faithful guardian. A faithful guardian so fearful in appearance that no other creature, however evil, would have dared to approach them.

Tymmon smiled then, a lopsided, mock-the-devil smile like the one that Komus used to suggest that something was only amusing on one side and more or less disastrous on the other. As in a case where a faithful guardian perhaps saves one from other dangers but also consumes the last of one's food supply, leaving one on the brink of starvation.

It was with some relief—but also with a strangely deep feeling of loss, and not just for the salted beef—that Tymmon went about the business of preparing to move on. Retrieving his articles of clothing from where he had spread them out to dry, he stacked them on the linen pack cover and collected his other belongings, the knife, the ax, the rope, the tinderbox, the flute—and then the cap and bells. Komus's jester's cap.

Komus. The memory was a sharp and rending pain. Where was he now and how was he faring? The thought of his father in captivity, perhaps hungry or in pain, caused Tymmon's throat to tighten and a hot and aching fire to rage behind his eyes. And after the pain, as usual, there came anger.

Anger at his own helplessness, at first. Anger that there was no way that he could help his father. No way to help him—and not even the hope that he might someday take revenge against his captors, which he would surely have done had he, Tymmon, been destined for knighthood. Destined for knighthood as he might have been if only Komus had not . . . He twisted the cap in his hands and threw it angrily to the ground—and then, as quickly, picked it up again. He was about to add it to his pile of belongings when another thought occurred to him.

Komus's colorful jester's cap, with its red, orange, and purple horns, was well known in all of Austerneve. So it followed that to take it with him might increase the danger he would surely be facing if Black Helmet's men had visited the villages and farms that lay to the south.

"What?" he imagined himself saying to a suspicious villager. "Am I the fugitive son of Komus, the court jester of Austerneve? No, of course not. I am only Arn (or some such name), born a baker's son though now an orphan."

Yes, with his usual quick-wittedness, he might well think of something of the sort to say. And then all might be well—until some less trusting townsman insisted on searching his belongings—and there found *the cap and bells.* No, it would be too dangerous a thing to carry. And God only knew why he brought it with him in the first place.

He was still musing on such things, turning the jester's cap in his hands and listening, perhaps for the last time, to the chiming bells when, from just behind him, there came a sudden sound—a strange mumbling grunt like someone trying to speak with his mouth full. Whirling around, Tymmon saw Troff emerging from the underbrush at the other side of the grove with something in his jaws.

Dropping the jester's cap at his feet, Tymmon gasped in surprise and consternation. He had, in just that little time, forgotten how huge the creature was—and how ugly. And then he saw what it was that Troff was holding in his mouth and gasped again. The object in the gargoyle's mouth was a fine fat pheasant.

"For—us?" Tymmon asked in a voice that he could not keep from quavering in anticipation.

Troff trotted across the clearing and dropped the bird at Tymmon's feet. With his great head hanging low, he continued to stare at the dead bird, making a soft growling noise in his throat and twitching the end of his tail.

Then he backed away, looked up into Tymmon's face, and clearly said that it was, indeed, for both of them.

And in just the time it took for Tymmon to pluck and clean the bird, and roast it over a newly built fire, he was eating one of the most important meals of his life. Eating and sharing the rich meat with Troff, the skillful hunter, the faithful guardian, the—whatever else he really was.

"Gargoyle?" Tymmon asked him once with his mouth full of pheasant. And the creature licked his chops, grinned, and tossed his great round head.

"Troff," he said, and Tymmon grinned back and repeated, "Troff, the gargoyle."

When the feast was over they lay for a while before the fire, but then Troff stirred restlessly, got up, and began to wander about the clearing. Stopping at a hollow that had recently held rainwater, he snuffled at the damp leaves, pawed at the earth, and snuffled again. Then he trotted back to Tymmon and stared urgently into his face.

"Thirsty?" Tymmon asked. "I know. I am too. Where can we find water?"

Troff turned and trotted off to the west, and jumping up, Tymmon grabbed his pack and followed. Halfway across the clearing he stopped, ran back, and retrieving the belled cap from where it had fallen, stuffed it deep into the pack. Then he ran to catch up.

Beyond the clearing they plunged into dense forest— and the endless network of trails that Tymmon remembered all too well. Faint, narrow footpaths that wound in every direction between towering trees, beds of fern and flowers, and dense thickets of underbrush.

Again, as on his previous visit to the Sombrous Forest,

Tymmon's mind raced faster than his feet, imagining dreadful things. Imagining all the dangers he had so often heard about—wolves in the underbrush, robbers lying in wait behind tree trunks, and harpies roosting overhead. Time and again, gasping at some newly envisioned horror, he thought to turn back. But they had already gone too far, too far to hope that he could find his way back to their starting place in the clearing. No, his only hope was Troff, and that was but a faint one, since he had no idea where, and to what, the gargoyle was leading him.

Once when the path became a narrow canyon between high walls of underbrush, Tymmon hesitated, and in doing so lost sight of his fast-moving guide. For a moment he was overcome by panic, but when he called in a voice pinched by fear, "Troff. Troff, come back," the gargoyle returned, trotting up to Tymmon and staring into his face with his furry forehead creased into furrows of concern.

But when he asked what was wrong, Tymmon, embarrassed at his own lack of courage, answered briefly and grumpily. "Nothing. Nothing, except you are going much too fast. Wait for me."

They went on then at a slightly slower pace for what seemed a great distance, so that Tymmon could only wonder, and tremble with awe, at the thought of the trackless maze that seemed to have engulfed all the land, as endless as the heavenly firmament. His legs were weak and trembling with exhaustion by the time he began to be aware of the sound of flowing water. Soon afterwards they came out upon the bank of a wide river.

Tymmon built a fire that night on a thumb-shaped peninsula of land that projected out into a deep curve of the river—as far away from the close-crowding shadows of the forest as he could get. Above the curve the river ran still and deep, but just below, it spread out into wide shallows that rippled over rocks and around many small boulders.

That night there was plenty to drink, and together Tymmon and Troff trapped a large trout in the shallows and caught it. They drank and ate, and when night fell they lay by the fire and listened to the sound of the river —and talked. That is, Tymmon did most of the talking, but Troff listened and now and then commented briefly or asked a question.

Tymmon spoke first of the five armed men and how they had taken Komus away. Troff listened carefully while he told the whole frightening story, from the strange sound that had awakened him to the end, when Komus secretly warned him to leave Austerneve and then had been led away by the terrible knight in the black-snouted helmet and his four companions.

"One of them struck him," he added after a moment. "I did not see the blow but I heard it and I heard the one with the black helm threaten to do worse if they found he was lying to them when he said I had gone from Austerneve. I wish I knew where they took him—and why."

As he spoke the last words his voice, suddenly and without warning, became weak and quavery, and tears flooded his eyes. Angrily he brushed them away and covered his face with both hands. He hated tears, and embarrassed to be so weak and unmanly, he kept his face hidden until a hot, wet tongue caressed the back of his hands. He jerked them away just as the tongue came again —up his cheek and across one eye. Tymmon drew back, wiping his face with his sleeve. Troff was regarding him anxiously, as one might a crying infant. Tymmon felt shamed—and angry.

"It didn't have to be that way," he cried. "It was his own fault." Troff drew back, looking startled and puzzled.

"It was. He didn't have to be a poor helpless minstrel and jester. My father was born to a noble family and he became a commoner by his own choice and action. He denied his birthright and left his homeland and country forever. He told me so himself."

Troff's expression showed that he was as amazed and incredulous as any human being would be to hear of such an incredible act of folly.

"I know," Tymmon said. "I would not have believed it myself except that he would never lie to me. So even though he would not explain, I . . ." Tymmon's mind went back to that day, almost a year ago, when his father had, in an unguarded moment, revealed his strange story.

Tymmon had been pressing his father to explain how he, a poor commoner, was skilled in reading and writing and in many other arts and sciences. His skills and learning, he told Tymmon impatiently, were due to the fact that he had been born to a noble family. But he had chosen as a young man to deny his birthright and leave the place of his birth. Just that much Komus said, but when Tymmon, almost overcome with delight and curiosity, had questioned him further, he had set his jaw, his eyes had darkened, and he would say no more.

"He told me only that much, and swore it was the truth. He would not tell me more. Nothing except that he was born to a noble family in the kingdom of Nordencor.

Oh yes, and that when my mother died of a fever—I was but two years old—he took me and set out to travel the world as a minstrel. As a common jongleur and minstrel. And when we came to Austerneve he took service in King Austern's court. He would say no more on that day, or on any day thereafter no matter how I pleaded. But he made me promise to tell no one. He especially made me promise I would not tell Lonfar. Although, in truth, I was no longer a friend to Lonfar at the time, and I certainly would not have told him. Although—although I would have greatly liked for him to know."

Troff stared at him, and then looked away indifferently, as if he had decided the matter was of little importance. It was clear that he did not understand how heartless it was of Komus to tell that much and then to refuse to say more. How cruel to even refuse to answer the question "Why?" To refuse to tell why he had chosen, not only for himself but for his son as well, the life of a commoner. And how particularly cruel it was to one who, like Tymmon, had special reasons to be all too aware of the vast difference between the future life of one born to the knighthood and one who was but the lowly offspring of a court jester.

"Do you know what a court jester is?" he asked Troff. And when the gargoyle seemed uncertain he went on angrily. "A court jester is a fool. A clown to be laughed at and made the butt of jokes." Tymmon could hear his own voice rising to an angry screech. He breathed deeply, swallowed hard, and went on, but the screech quickly returned. "A court jester is a buffoon who spends his life pleasing stupid people by making them feel superior to the pitiful and craven fool he is pretending to be. Only pretending because—as God himself knows well, and all men should know too—my father truly is more gifted and wiser and more learned than any other man in Austerneve could ever hope to . . ."

The tears returned and Tymmon threw himself down on his blanket and buried his face in his arms, and when Troff snuffled in his ear and pushed at his hand with his ugly snout, he told him gruffly to go away.

SIX

I t was better during the day. Better because there was little time for thought or remembrance. Tymmon soon found that in the hours between sunrise and sundown it was not difficult to keep his mind on the events of the moment, and to how those events related to the condition of his stomach.

The struggle for food was constant and endless. In the first few days they moved their base constantly, traveling always southward along the riverbank, always looking for a sheltered camping spot and for better fishing and hunting. But even on the days when the hunting had been successful they seldom ate more than once, and it seemed they were always hungry. Sometimes when their luck had been good Tymmon tried to save something for the next day, but that proved to be impossible. Troff never stopped eating until everything—the last scrap of burned skin, and even the last small bone—had disappeared. Obviously a gargoyle's belly was as boundless and endless as the sea.

Of course, it was Troff who brought in most of what they ate, partridges and water birds, and once a fine fat rabbit. But Tymmon was soon able to do his part. With a lance fashioned from a long straight branch he occasionally managed, after long hours of trial and error, to spear a fish in the river shallows. Now and then he found a few nuts left over from the autumn before, and on one lucky day he found a nest of duck eggs that were very tasty when roasted in the ashes of a fire.

But while Troff ranged into the depths of the forest on his hunting trips, Tymmon's expeditions, whether to look for food or gather wood for the fire, were always limited to the riverbank and to short distances from the camp. There, on the bank, where the river stretched away to the north and south in a broad path that could be followed until it would undoubtedly come at last to civilization, he felt safer and more at ease. But even there he could always feel it—around and behind him. The dim, deep Sombrous waiting to ensnare him in its endless, haunted maze. Even later, when they had decided on a more permanent base, and it had become necessary to collect saplings and fern fronds to build a hut, he went only a few yards into the forest, or waited until Troff could accompany him.

The hut was begun after several days of travel and nights of sleeping beside an open fire. The rain had returned then, and with it more long hours of soggy misery. It was after such a wet and chilly night that Tymmon began to construct a shelter near the foot of a sloping stretch of sandy beach. A three-sided lean-to, roofed with reeds and fern fronds, its walls no more than a palisade of stakes cut from young saplings. The flimsy walls slowed the advance of the north wind but little, and the roof dripped in the worst downpours, but it was better than no shelter at all. During the dark nights, curled in his blanket with Troff at his feet and the fire before them, it was a comfort to have a wall behind his back. A barrier, however rickety, between him and the forest.

So the days rushed by, but the nights seemed to last forever. If he had not known that it was impossible, Tymmon would have been sure that the hours of darkness in the Sombrous Forest were longer than they were elsewhere. Long after the fire burned low and Troff slept soundly, he was often wide awake. Wide awake, thinking and remembering, and listening to the forest sounds that he could sometimes hear over the soft liquid mumblings of the river.

Sometimes there were screams or howls. Soon after sundown and again in the first dim light of day, a high moaning wail would suddenly shatter the soft, pure silence of the morning air. A wild tormented sound, sadder and more pitiful than the keening of any human mourner. But even more terrifying were the noises that came in the depths of the night—deep throbbing cries punctuated by sharp high-pitched yelps. Clearly the baying of the wolves of the Sombrous, horrible sharp-fanged beasts known throughout the North Countries for their ferocity and greedy hunger. Staring into the darkness, his ears straining, Tymmon sometimes prodded Troff with his foot, and told him to awake and listen.

The first few times he was thus aroused Troff came alert quickly and hearkened, but after a bit he seemed to take little interest, even when the terrible wails came again and again. Sometimes he only looked at Tymmon reproachfully and turned away, and even when the baying of the wolves seemed very near he only growled softly and then yawned, stretched, and said there was nothing to fear while he was there. Then he went back to sleep.

But after Tymmon had prodded him into wakefulness several times he became harder and harder to awaken, only lifting his head briefly, snorting and mumbling, and then sinking back into a motionless and useless lump at Tymmon's feet. That, at least, was his reaction unless Tymmon was able to get his attention and keep it—in one of several ways. Tymmon soon learned which ways were most useful.

The old flute had been a gift from Komus, and Tymmon had learned to play it when he was no more than four years of age. "My father taught me," he told Troff, turning the beautifully fashioned instrument in his hands, "although he said I needed very little teaching, having been born, as he was, with a true ear and a quick memory. Sometimes during those years I even played in the great hall before King Austern and his guests."

Troff seemed impressed. Tymmon shrugged. "I remember it but little. I was, I suppose, a kind of curiosity, having so much skill at a tender age. I have not played now for many years."

But the old tunes came back and Troff clearly enjoyed

them, turning his head from side to side to listen and now and then lifting his muzzle toward the heavens and join-ing in—in a low throbbing lament, somewhat like the wailing of the wolves.

He liked the merry songs, too, particularly the lively rollicking chansonettes and folk tunes that Komus had played and sung to entertain King Austern's guests in the great hall. And to these merrier tunes Troff sang in a different way, adding bursts of short staccato syllables to his usual quavering themes. The music and singing worked well, but when Tymmon tired of making music, he found that Troff could also be kept awake by the tell-ing of stories.

Many of the tales, also, had been part of Komus's reper-toire, which Tymmon had learned by listening to his fa-ther's rehearsals. Komus had spent long hours practicing dramatic effects, the miming and capering and mimicking that he would use to enliven the tales for his noble audi-ence. The king's guests, Komus had said, enjoyed his comic antics, and Troff seemed to appreciate such things also, when they were related and even embellished and improved upon by Tymmon, who, like his father, had a gift for mimicry and farce.

Some of Komus's stories were exciting accounts of the brave deeds of famous heroes, heroes not only of recent times but also of ancient Greece and Rome. Others were romantic tales of pure and chivalrous love, and still others were lively and humorous stories concerning heroes who were not always so pure and noble.

Troff listened politely to such tales, but sometimes his attention wandered and his eyelids drooped. He seemed to like better the true accounts of Tymmon's own past. Particularly, he seemed to enjoy hearing about Lonfar and the many adventures he and Tymmon had shared.

"We were friends for many years," Tymmon told him. Shutting out more recent memories, he could feel himself smiling as he recalled all the good times. Troff smiled, too, thumping his tufted tail and lolling his tongue. "Yes, for many years. I think we were less than five years old—we were of almost exactly the same age—when Sir Hildar first brought Lonfar to Komus for instruction. I did not question it then, but I suppose there were those who did. And truly one would not expect a noble knight to send his son to be taught by a jester. But the priest at Austerneve at that time, Father Nominus, was very old and of unsound mind, and there were few in the castle who could read and write. So my father taught us—Lonfar and me together—and we learned to read and write and do sums, and to enjoy each other's company as well."

Troff seemed to like best stories concerning the games that Tymmon and Lonfar had played—games of high adventure that were played in empty attics, crumbling turrets, and forgotten dungeons. And no matter how dulleyed the sleepy beast had been only a moment before, he quickly became alert and attentive when Tymmon leaped to his feet to demonstrate the wooden sword battles and broomstick jousts that he and Lonfar had often staged in the castle courtyard.

"We were together from dawn until dusk in those years," he told Troff. "So much so that the people of the castle, nobles and commoners alike, began to speak our names together. Tymmon-and-Lonfar or Lonfar-and-Tymmon—as if they were but one word. Some even said we looked alike, except for our coloring, since Lonfar is not dark as I am, but very pale with hair the exact hue of harvest grain. We were, in truth, closer than brothers, Lonfar and I, until . . ."

Tymmon stopped, and Troff, who had been thoughtfully licking one of his great front paws, looked up quickly.

Tymmon shrugged. "Well, until after Lonfar became a page and started his training for knighthood. Oh, he swore it would make no difference, and right at first it did not. When his training in horsemanship and fencing began, I would meet him afterwards and he would teach me what he had learned. And sometimes I was even allowed to go with him to the archery master and practice with bow and arrow. But then—well, then—only last year a new knight came to Austerneve. The baronet Quantor, son of Lord Krodon, baron of Unterrike."

Tymmon pronounced the names with a flourish, indicating how important they were, but Troff took little notice. "Surely you have heard of Unterrike?" Tymmon asked.

Troff looked away and stared thoughtfully into space before his great round eyes returned questioningly to Tymmon. "Unterrike?"

"It is a large fief, a dominion. Bordering Austerneve to the southwest. And the baron is a highborn lord—one of the richest and most powerful in all the North Countries. So, as I was saying, the baron's son, Baronet Quantor of Unterrike, came to do service in King Austern's court. And soon after, Lonfar learned that when he reached the age of fourteen he would be pledged to Quantor as squire. And that made all the difference in the world."

Troff looked puzzled.

"Well, I should think it would be very clear. Unterrike is one of the greatest kingdoms in all the North Countries, and Baron Krodon the most powerful lord. Of course he is not from an ancient and honored line as is King Austern, but Unterrike barons have always supported a large number of knights who were unlanded but known for their skill in warfare. And of course, in the days before the High King united all the North Countries, Unterrike was Austerneve's greatest enemy. The barons' armies often attacked Austerneve Castle and laid waste the countryside. The village of Qweasle, at the foot of the tor, was burned and sacked more than once by the forces of Unterrike. But now Baron Krodon has become King Austern's honored friend, and his son, the baronet Quantor, has come to serve in King Austern's court."

Troff was listening attentively now, his head tipped to one side, which always tended to give him a reasonable and intelligent air.

"So you can understand why Sir Hildar was greatly pleased and honored when the baronet agreed to take his son, Lonfar, as squire. And Lonfar was also. He began to spend much of his time serving the baronet, even though he will not be old enough to pledge as his squire for more than a year."

Tymmon stopped and shrugged and then sighed and shrugged again. "So that was it. It seemed the baronet felt it was not suitable for his future squire to spend so much of his time with a commoner—the son of a jester. And, it seems, Lonfar agreed with him. We have not so much as spoken together in more than a year."

Troff growled softly and said he did not like that part of the story. Then he rolled over on his side and closed his eyes.

"A song then," Tymmon said quickly. "I shall sing another song. A lively one. Shall I sing 'The Knight of the Honorable Name'?"

Troff thumped his tail and opened one eye, so Tymmon jumped to his feet and built up the fire. And when the flames were again leaping as high and bright as did the torches in the great hall when Komus was performing, he began. Just as Komus had always done, he entered with an acrobatic caper that carried him onto the stage in a series of spins and twirls and tumbles and ended with a grand gesture.

"If I may have your attention, most excellent and exquisite lords and ladies, I will now entertain you with a sweet ballad composed by that widely renowned troubadour, Hulf of Mundgross."

Still holding the pose, he stopped to explain, in case Troff had forgotten. "Actually he wrote the song himself. As far as I know there's no such person as Hulf of Mundgross. And so—lords and ladies, 'The Knight of the Honorable Name.' "

The song had many verses, each of them telling the story of one of the knight's chivalrous deeds, such as slaying dragons, saving damsels in distress, and helping comrades in arms who had been accused of horrible crimes by killing their accusers in trial by battle. And between each of the verses there was a catchy refrain which Komus had always sung while pacing grandly around the stage in a stately manner, as one might in some great and solemn procession:

Let us sing of a knight of great valor and fame,
Sir Bloodspiller Bergburner, Lord of No Shame.
Let us sing of the glory, of the deeds grand and gory,
Of the Knight of the Honorable Name.

Troff liked the refrain and the procession, but during the verses, which were quite long and wordy, he sometimes lost interest. Lowering his big ugly head onto his paws, he dutifully kept his eyelids partly open and rolled his eyes sleepily in Tymmon's direction.

At last Tymmon discarded his entertainer's pose and dropped down in front of his inattentive audience. "You are just not listening carefully," he said sternly. "The verses are most amusing, if you grasp their meaning. As in the one about the dragon. When the knight and all his squires and pages arrive in the village that is being harassed by the dragon, the villagers have to feed and house their rescuers. And before the dragon is finally killed, the knight and his party have eaten everything and laid waste the countryside, and all the villagers have died of starvation. And then the great knight leaves, so proud of slaying the dragon he doesn't even notice that the people he came to save have all starved to death. The ending is meant to be a satire, a kind of mockery. Don't you understand?"

Troff grinned and lolled his tongue and then rolled over on his back and asked Tymmon to scratch his belly. By the time the scratching was finished, Tymmon noticed that the sky had begun to lighten and the strange night-time noises had given way to the first sleepy chirping of birds.

Tymmon crawled under his blanket. He could sleep now. But before he closed his eyes he found his thoughts returning briefly to what he had just told Troff. "A kind of mockery," he had said. He had not really thought of it in just that way before. But suddenly it seemed to be true. Seen in a certain way, many of Komus's songs and stories as well had been a kind of mockery. This sudden realization seemed important, but before he could explore it further it clouded into dreams.

I'll think on it more tomorrow, he told himself, but when he awakened, the sun was already high in the sky, and there was much to be done. Troff had already gone hunting.

SEVEN

A s the days passed, Tymmon thought more and more often of leaving the forest and, in spite of the danger from Black Helmet and his men, returning to the farms and villages of the valley.

"The Sombrous may be all very well for you," he told Troff. "But human beings need to be with their own kind. It is most necessary for people to be with other people. And then there is the matter of food. I know that lions and other such wild beasts can live on nothing but the flesh of their prey, and I suppose that gargoyles are much the same. But humans need a variety of foods in order to thrive and stay in good health. There is, for instance, bread."

Bread had, of late, haunted his dreams. Bread in particular but also porridge, cheese, soups and stews, dumplings, puddings, and pies. And now that spring was here and the days warming, there would soon be fresh fruits and vegetables. His hunger for such things filled his dreams with wonderful feasts of the past.

Sleeping, he once more tasted the ripe cherries he and Lonfar had picked in the orchard of a Qweasle farmer. In other dreams he once again enjoyed the delicious things to be found in the castle kitchen, where he and Lonfar had often been treated by the good-natured cooks. Not to mention the wonderful meals he and his father had often eaten late at night after Komus returned from entertaining King Austern's guests, bringing with him a great basket of strange and wonderful food—leftovers from the king's banquets. Even the simple porridge he himself often prepared in the three-legged stewpot on their own hearth became a regular feature of his nightly imaginings.

But food was, of course, not the most important reason Tymmon felt driven to move on. There was another constant yearning even more deep and basic than the need for food and human companionship, and that was his need for some word of his father. Even if there was nothing he could do to rescue him, he yearned to discover where he had been taken, and why.

It was an impossible dream, he told himself. Even to dream that he might hear word of Komus was hopeless—and dangerous. Dangerous because the search for news would surely lead back to Austerneve—where Black Helmet and his men would most certainly be lying in wait. But the fantasy persisted—that somehow he might rescue his father or, at least, at some future time, discover the identity of his captors and punish them for their evil deed.

The last was, indeed, a forlorn and hopeless fantasy, but over the weeks in the Sombrous it had begun to mingle with an older flight of imagination that had begun soon after Komus had let slip the truth about his noble birth. A fantastical plan for the future in which Tymmon saw himself one day returning to his birthplace, to the city of Nordencor, where he would reclaim the honorable position that was rightfully his, and then someday return to Austerneve as a knight, famed throughout the North Countries for his valor and skill in battle.

But now that older dream had lengthened to include further scenes in which Tymmon, a knighted nobleman of Nordencor, was going forth with page and squire to find his father's captors and vanquish them in honorable combat.

It was, indeed, a far and distant dream. Nordencor was many leagues to the south, and certainly Tymmon had not originally planned to make his pilgrimage there at such an early age. But now that he had been forced by fate to leave Austerneve, why should he not head south, in the direction of Nordencor and his birthright?

But there were other matters to consider, among them the problem of Troff. If Tymmon did in fact decide to make his way out of the forest and onto the highroad, what would he do about Troff? It would be wonderful if he were able to take the gargoyle with him. Wonderful, but quite obviously impossible.

Tymmon looked at the gargoyle, who was, at the moment, lying beside him on the riverbank. It was a warm afternoon, almost like summer, and they were resting after a tough and gamy meal of roasted heron. Troff was lying on his back with his feet in the air. With his great round head turned upside down, his floppy jowls fell back, exposing his sharp white teeth. Except for the teeth, which were fairly alarming from whatever angle they happened to be seen, he did not at the moment seem at all intimidating. But still, it was impossible to imagine the effect such a strange creature might have on the inhabitants of farm and village. Simple peasant folk who were, as Komus often said, beset by so many superstitions that every change in the weather was taken as the work of supernatural beings, evil or otherwise.

"Have you ever shown yourself to other human beings?" Tymmon asked.

Troff rolled the one eye that Tymmon could see and said quite clearly that, yes, he had. The one eye rolled again, the tufted tail thumped the ground, and changing the subject, he asked for another scratch.

Tymmon sighed and scratched the furry belly, and Troff, a hind foot twitching, grunted in satisfaction. But Tymmon wasn't convinced by Troff's answer. There had not been, as far as he knew, any rumors of living gargoyles invading the North Countries, as there surely would have been if such a creature had been widely seen. It seemed more likely that Troff had not understood the question or didn't care to answer it honestly. After a few moments Tymmon asked another, and more important, question.

"If I were to leave the forest and travel southward along the highway, what would you do?"

Troff quickly turned himself right side up and stared at Tymmon from under a furred and furrowed brow.

"It would be impossible, I'm afraid, for you to go with

me. If a creature enchanted into life from cold hard stone appeared among the villagers, there would surely be panic in the streets. And I might well be suspected of being the conjurer who brought you to life. And quite possibly burned at the stake as a warlock, or even a disciple of the devil."

Burned at the stake. Tymmon remembered many tales of witch burnings. He had often heard of one that had occurred in Austerneve many years ago. And in other nearby fiefdoms there had been several such events in the not too distant past. Komus himself had once spoken of how a young woman had fallen under suspicion simply because she loved animals. All animals, even the wild things of the forest, and was beloved by them in return. Tymmon did not know if the young woman had been burned as a witch, because Komus had broken off the telling of the story before it ended and would not return to it.

But the half-told tale had returned to his memory often like the haunting memory of an unfinished dream. And now it occurred to him that if a person could be accused of witchcraft because of friendships with owls and hares, what would be the fate of someone who was the friend of a gargoyle?

"No, I fear that when we leave here we must go our separate ways," Tymmon said sadly, and Troff crawled forward on his belly, making a pitiful moaning noise deep in his throat.

"Well, never mind," Tymmon hurried to reassure him. "I'm not going immediately. I'm just thinking about it."

But it was on the very next day that something happened that turned thinking into action. Immediate action.

It was midmorning of the following day and Troff had gone hunting sometime before. Tymmon had washed his doublet and jerkin and spread them out to dry on the riverbank and added a few new reeds to the thatching of the hut's roof. The gathering of firewood for the coming night would come next, a chore that was daily becoming more difficult.

When Tymmon and Troff had first arrived at this particular camping place, there had seemed to be an endless supply of firewood. But now all the driftwood deposited by past floods, as well as the deadfall at the edge of the forest, had been burned. Scouting again among the tall trees that grew near the river, Tymmon found nothing except a few pieces suitable for kindling. At last he decided that today he would have to do something that he had carefully avoided until that time. He would have to go farther, following one of the trails that wound its way into the depths of the forest.

His knife and ax in his belt, he set out, choosing a pathway at random. He moved slowly, stopping often to mark his trail by bending saplings or cutting blazes into the trunks of trees. And stopping also to look and listen —to stare for long silent moments down the dim leafy corridors, and up into the thick branches overhanging his head.

He continued in that cautious manner for some time before he came upon a lucky find—a large fallen tree with many long thick limbs—enough dry firewood for several nights. Although he remained alert and watchful as he cut and trimmed the branches, he saw and heard nothing unusual, and it was not long before he had collected a neat stack of logs as long and thick as a man's arm. On the return trip he followed his blazed trail with no difficulty. He was almost back to the riverbank, and congratulating himself on his bravery and skill as a forester, when he heard the voices.

There were two of them. Crouching behind a thicket at the edge of the forest, Tymmon watched as two shaggy-haired men pulled a small boat through the shallows and up onto the bank. As they came closer he could see that they were dressed in dirty and ragged homespun smocks and leggings. The one in the lead was small and wiry with a sharp pointed face and deep-set eyes, while the second was tall and heavily built, but slow-moving and with a blurred, dull-eyed countenance that did not speak highly of his intelligence.

At first Tymmon was not greatly concerned, thinking them to be fishermen from a nearby village. He was even, for a brief moment, considering greeting them and asking them for directions to their village—in case he did decide, at some point in the future, to make his way back to the open land of the valley.

But as he hesitated, the men completed the beaching of their boat and turned to look up the bank toward Tymmon's hut. And then, as they started up the slope, the slight, wiry one drew a long evil-looking dagger from a sheath at his belt.

It was not that the man armed himself that was so terrifying. Anyone, even an honest village fisherman, might well prepare for trouble before venturing to explore a hut in the wilderness. But this weapon was finely made of bright Spanish steel, its hilt inlaid with gold and silver and precious gems—clearly not the weapon of a peasant or fisherman. And the other man, who carried with him a crude metal-headed club, was wearing on his large feet beautifully crafted leather boots with curling pointed toes. Both men were clearly outlaws since, by decree of the High King, any commoner in possession of precious metals, or even shoes with pointed toes, was guilty of a criminal offense.

Suddenly it was all too clear. These men were brigands, members of one of the robber bands, who made their living by robbing and murdering. And it was also clear that the boots and dagger were stolen goods, probably taken from murdered victims of noble birth.

Chilled by the sudden realization that he was in terrible danger, Tymmon crouched lower behind the thicket and watched as the two cutthroats climbed up the slope. They said nothing until they neared the firepit, when the one in the lead stopped and spoke.

"Stay there, Obam, and keep your eyes on the woods. I will see what we have here."

The big man turned to stare directly at Tymmon's thicket and he ducked lower, so that he did not see the small man enter the hut. But a moment later, when he cautiously raised his head, the big man had turned away to watch as his companion emerged carrying Tymmon's blanket and tinderbox. The small brigand glanced at the dirty ragged blanket and threw it aside, and was examining the tinderbox when the other called, "What be that, Jagg? What you got there?"

"Nothing of worth. 'Tis likely the camp of a runaway serf. Come. Let's be off." Carrying the tinderbox, he started back toward the river, but the other, instead of following, turned aside, hung his club from a loop on his belt, and crawled into the lean-to. When he, too, emerged and started down the slope to the river he was grinning widely and staring at something he carried in both his huge dirty hands. It was Komus's cap and bells.

The loss of the tinderbox, which would mean cold, dark nights and meals of raw flesh, had made Tymmon's throat tighten with pain and rage, but somehow the stolen cap was much harder to bear. Clutching his head with both hands, he was clenching his teeth against a shriek of angry protest when, from directly behind him, a bloodcurdling sound made him leap to his feet in terror. His confused and panic-stricken mind had barely noted the source of the deep threatening roar when Troff bounded past him and out onto the riverbank.

Tymmon could only watch in stunned amazement as Troff, still making the terrifying sound, dashed straight at the smaller brigand, who had dropped the tinderbox and was trying to pull his dagger from its sheath. The charging gargoyle crashed at full speed into the cutthroat's chest, sending him sprawling backward, and a moment later Troff was standing over the fallen man clutching his arm in his jaws. "Help!" the brigand screamed. "Help me, Obam, you fool. Club him. Club the beast."

The bigger man, who had been standing motionless, as if paralyzed by astonishment, began to creep forward brandishing his heavy club. But at that moment Tymmon, too, came alive and, grabbing up a length of firewood, ran down the bank and reached the second thief just as he was raising his club over Troff's head. Intent on the noisy scene in front of him, the man was not even aware of Tymmon's approach until the heavy log smashed into his arm.

Afterwards the order of the events that followed became blurred in Tymmon's mind, but he did recall that at some point he had tugged at the loose skin on the back of Troff's neck, asking him to release his grip on the smaller man's arm. And shortly thereafter both of the brigands were staggering down to their boat, moaning and cursing, while Tymmon stood beside Troff on the bank with the club, the dagger, and the tinderbox lying near their feet. And clutched in Tymmon's right hand was the jester's cap.

At that point the pace of events became much slower, since neither of the robbers seemed able to make any use of their right arms, and it took them some time to drag their boat into the river and push off from shore. During that time they turned their heads often to stare angrily, and anxiously, at Troff and Tymmon, but they said nothing at all except to curse each other's clumsiness. But once out into the stream they became much more talkative.

"You are not rid of us," the smaller man shouted. "We be back soon for your worthless hides."

"And for my mace," the big man bellowed. "We be back for my mace and Jagg's dagger. And we be bringing the others with us with swords and crossbows. Will we not be, Jagg?"

"Shut up, Obam," the other said, and then lowered his voice, but his words carried well over the narrow strip of water. "We be back soon enough but not with the company. We be saying naught to the company. Do you hear me, Obam? Do you want them all to know that Jagg and Obam be beaten by a boy and a dog?"

When the men and the boat had disappeared down the river, Troff turned suddenly and disappeared into the forest, to return almost immediately carrying a dead pheasant, which he undoubtedly had been bringing back to the camp when he became aware of the presence of the robbers. As Tymmon built up the fire and cleaned and roasted the bird he said little, but his mind was busy. Troff, too, seemed nervous and restless. It wasn't until the meal was finished that Tymmon spoke.

"We will have to leave," he told Troff. "Sooner or later they will send others against us, or return themselves. However, I do not think they will return alone until their wounds have healed, and that may take some time."

He paused, grinning. "We did well, Troff. I surely broke the right arm of the big one, and I fear you left the other in even worse condition. It is not to be wondered at that they were reluctant to tell their companions the truth of our encounter. That they, two armed men, were so bested by a boy and . . ."

Tymmon stopped, suddenly recalling the exact words of the smaller outlaw. A dog! The brigand had called Troff a dog. In the heat of the moment the word had been without significance, but now . . . He turned quickly to look at Troff, who had just curled his great thick body into a ridiculous position as he attempted to scratch the back of his head.

"Troff!" Tymmon said, accusingly. "A dog?"

Troff stopped scratching. Hanging his head he looked up at Tymmon from the tops of his eyes, in a manner that spoke openly of a guilty conscience.

Tymmon frowned. "Are you then only a dog?" he asked in angry amazement.

Troff leaped to his feet, lunged at Tymmon, and with a playful nudge nearly knocked him off his feet. Then, as he cavorted in a circle, he said that he was Troff. Not a dog, but Troff. Troff, Troff, Troff. Then he turned his back, lay down, and began to lick a front foot, pretending not to notice as Tymmon walked slowly around him.

How could he be only a dog? For one thing he was a great deal larger and uglier than any dog that Tymmon had ever seen. Dogs, in Tymmon's experience, were all fairly similar. In fact there had been, at Austerneve Castle, only coursing hounds, small light-bodied beasts with delicate narrow heads and long thin legs. He had heard of course of other breeds, large sleek-bodied beasts used in the eastern forests for the hunting of boar; and others— squat, big-headed, flat-faced animals bred for the baiting of bulls. But at Austerneve the old king had long ago banished all other breeds to preserve the purity of his favorites, the swift and graceful hounds used for the coursing of rabbits and other small game. It would take three or four coursing hounds to weigh as much as Troff. And as to appearance—there were few similarities, except for such generalities as a tail and four legs.

And then, of course, there was Troff's ability to speak. And he did speak to Tymmon, there was no doubt of that. Not, perhaps, in the usual manner, but there was no doubt that he understood everything that Tymmon said.

At least, when he wished to. And in his own way, was he not able to clearly and without question make his thoughts and wishes known?

"You do speak to me, don't you?" Tymmon asked, and looking up, Troff cocked his head thoughtfully. "You have spoken to me clearly from that first night when you appeared out of the darkness. And you understand everything I say, don't you, Troff?"

Suddenly Troff jumped up, stood on his hind legs and, placing his front feet on Tymmon's shoulders, licked him sloppily from chin to brow. Staring into Tymmon's eyes, he said with great clarity and assurance that he understood everything very well indeed.

Tymmon wiped his face with his sleeve. "And you are a gargoyle?"

The tongue licked again, this time up Tymmon's neck and over his ear, as he hastily turned away his face. And then Troff said that he was a gargoyle. Yes, certainly, a gargoyle.

Tymmon sighed. "Yes, I was afraid so," he said. And aware of what tomorrow must bring he was suddenly weighted by a deep and heavy burden of sorrow and loneliness.

EIGHT

I t was a long night, full of anxious dreams as well as long periods of wakefulness during which Tymmon planned and worried and planned again.

At first he firmly resolved to stay with Troff in the forest, at least until the end of summer. Not here in this camp, since it was now known to the brigands, but perhaps farther south along the bank of the river. Yes, he would stay with Troff at least a little while longer.

But later, during the deep still hours, his plans changed again. He would have to leave, and very soon. He could not continue to live without human companionship, and with no food but the flesh of wild game. But most of all he could not help but follow the hope, however faint, that once back among mankind he would somehow hear news of his father.

Yes, he and Troff would have to part, he decided sadly. But as sleep came nearer and his thoughts drifted into fragmented fantasies, he was at least able to console himself with scenes in which he was traveling south to Nordencor—and then meeting his father's friends and relatives, who were greeting him warmly and then . . .

At that point his plans drifted into a dream in which Sir Tymmon of Nordencor, a man now and a knight, well armed and mounted on a fiery steed, was storming some evil stronghold in which his father was being held prisoner.

But even when such distant dreams were banished with the approach of daylight, his last decision held. And with it came the sad knowledge that, when the day began, he would have to say good-bye to Troff and then, all alone, start his journey back to the homes of men.

Soon after daybreak he arose quietly and began to dress. Inside the lean-to Troff had awakened, but he was still sprawled across Tymmon's blanket. With his chin on his enormous paws he rolled his eyes to watch as Tymmon began to gather his belongings and once again tie them into a pack. Troff knew. It was clear that he knew, although Tymmon had not yet spoken of what he was planning to do.

Tymmon worked swiftly and with determination—and tried not to look at Troff. Even when it was necessary to retrieve his blanket by politely asking the gargoyle to rise, he tried to keep his eyes turned away. But somehow as he returned to his packing an image of drooping ears, sad eyes, and worried brow was still before him.

He would not look at Troff again, he decided as he

wrapped Komus's cap and bells and hid it deep within the pack. He would finish his preparations, and meanwhile he would keep his mind busy with other things. He would think only of his plan to follow the river, which would provide him with water to drink and perhaps an occasional fish to eat, as well as a path through the forest. A path that would surely lead eventually to the open land of farm and village. At last, the pack was completed, and he could put it off no longer. Turning to face the sad accusing eyes beneath the bulging gray-brown forehead, he said, "Well, Troff . . ."

His own eyes were suddenly hot and wet and he had to swallow hard before his voice could make its way around a burning lump that had suddenly leaped up to fill his throat.

"Well, Troff," he tried again. "It is very hard to say good-bye. You have saved my life many times over and I—I—" The lump grew, squeezing his voice into a high-pitched whine that ended in a painful gasp. He turned away quickly and, collapsing on the ground, buried his face in his hands.

He was struggling to hold back the tears when suddenly there was a hot breath on his face and then a heavy pressure on the left side of his body. Cracking his fingers he peered at Troff, who was now sitting close beside him, leaning heavily against his shoulder. Tymmon's arm went out, around the warm, hairy body, and for some time they sat without moving. And as they sat thus, a strange new revelation began to unfold itself gradually within Tymmon's mind.

The idea grew and expanded, and at last, without mov-

ing his head, he said, "Troff. I know I said that you could
not come with me when I go back to the homes of men—
for fear that you would be seen as an enchanted beast.
And I as a demon in league with the devil. But it has just
occurred to me to wonder if . . . Do you suppose that
there might be others who would consider you to be only
a dog, as did those two brigands?"

He again glanced at the gargoyle. " 'A dog,' I would say.
'Of course he is naught but a dog. What else might he be?'
And you of course would say nothing. It would not be
wise for you to let them know that you can speak."

He sat up suddenly and turned to face the creature
beside him—and for a moment his new resolve wavered.
He did look so like a monster. If not exactly a gargoyle,
certainly a creature of similar countenance. But at the
moment he was also looking much more like his usual
eager-eyed and grinning self. "Do you think it would be
possible?" Tymmon asked. "Do you think you could come
with me and play the part of a dog? Would you come with
me, Troff?"

At once Troff was on his feet, and bounding around
with such wild abandon that Tymmon was forced to
dodge here and there to keep from being trod upon.
When, at last, some measure of calm had been restored,
Tymmon said, "All right, then. You will be only a dog. We
will travel together and I shall tell those that we meet,
'This is my faithful dog, Troff.' We shall set off now, and
on the way I will counsel you on how to behave in a
doglike manner. I have just one more thing to do and
then we will go."

In the fire pit the ashes were cold and gray and the hut

was empty, except for the weapons left behind by the
fleeing cutthroats. Tymmon considered the club first, the
huge metal-headed mace which had belonged to the larger
of the brigands. Lifting it, he tried his arm against its
weight and, after a moment's consideration, walked to the
riverbank and, using both hands, threw it out as far as he
could into the current. As the club disappeared into the
water, Troff, who had followed him to the river's edge,
watched eagerly and with obvious approval.

Back in the hut Tymmon picked up the Spanish dagger.
The dagger was another matter entirely. It was a weapon
meant for a nobleman. A weapon such as might be presented as a gift of honor to a pledged squire and candidate
for knighthood, as Lonfar would soon be. And as he,
Tymmon, also might have been if Komus had not renounced his heritage.

Holding the glittering weapon in his hands gave Tymmon a feeling of power and pride. He tested its razor-
sharp blade with his thumb and then tried a practice
parry and thrust against an imaginary enemy. He stepped
backward, dodged a counterthrust, and advanced again—
and then suddenly froze. Troff had growled—an alarmingly fierce and threatening sound. As Tymmon lowered
the weapon the growl subsided, but the gargoyle's eyes did
not leave the dagger, and a muffled threat continued to
roll up from somewhere deep inside his thick chest.

"No," Tymmon said. "Why should I throw it away,
too? It's far too valuable and too beautiful. And what if
we are again attacked by brigands? We may well have need
of such a weapon. And besides, it is not as if I were un-
worthy to be armed in such a manner, like that lowborn

rascal we took it from. It is entirely suitable that I should own it, since I am, as I have told you, of noble birth. And besides, you are already forgetting that you are naught but a dog. A dog is a humble and obedient creature and not given to strong opinions."

Troff turned away then, pretending to have lost interest in the discussion, as he was wont to do when he was losing an argument. So Tymmon hung the dagger in his belt and shouldered his pack, and they set off southward along the riverbank.

As they made their way along sandy beaches and then among scattered boulders, Tymmon explained his plans for their journey. "At first I was thinking of trying to retrace our path back to the place where I entered the forest. But I am not at all certain that we could find our way, even now that you are with me. And even if we were able to find the place where we entered the forest, my troubles would not be over. We would come out into the valley not far from Qweasle, where everyone is sure to know of the reward offered by Black Helmet."

Tymmon paused as they scrambled up and over a small boulder that blocked their path and then, once more back on level land, continued. "But if we follow the river southward, we should come out of the forest near the city of Montreff. I have not been there, but I have heard that it is a journey of many days from Austerneve, and perhaps Black Helmet will not have traveled so far in his search for me." He did not go on to mention that Nordencor also lay to the south, and that at Montreff he would be well on the way to the city of his birth. Instead he only repeated that the large city of Montreff should be their first destination. "Do you not agree, Troff?" he asked.

There was no answer. Troff, who was staring toward the forest and sniffing the air, seemed to be preoccupied with other things. And as the day wore on he seemed, more and more often, to be tense and distant.

They walked all that day, through forest and meadow, keeping always within sight or sound of the river. Late in the day the land became more rugged and the river narrower and more rapid as it flowed through a gorge between rocky highlands. They paused only once at a likely fishing spot, where Tymmon managed to spear a small trout, and then pressed on until sunset, before they stopped to gather a large stack of driftwood, build a fire, and cook their meal. And although Troff's portion was surely not enough to satisfy his huge appetite, he showed no interest in leaving the campsite on a hunting expedition.

Twilight was deepening as Tymmon chose a sandy spot between two boulders near the river's edge, stacked a supply of firewood close at hand, spread his blanket, and then stretched out with Troff beside him, and the Spanish dagger near at hand. He was still hungry as well as being deeply, achingly weary, and sleep did not come easily.

It was a strange place. Around their camping spot, rugged boulder-strewn land sloped upward from the water's edge to heavily wooded hills. Here and there among the great gray stones dead trees leaned and tilted at crazy angles. Across the river a steep cliff of sheer rock rose straight up for many feet to a high plateau covered with stunted trees. The air was still and silent except for the liquid murmur of the deep running river, but the silence brought no feeling of peace and calm. Instead it seemed to be only a breathless hush, the tense and quiet wait before the storm, or perhaps the stillness that spreads across the land just before a hidden enemy launches a surprise attack.

Tymmon moved closer to Troff. Tonight, in this weird place where towering rock and skeleton tree cast ghostly shadows, he was glad—extremely glad—for Troff's large warm presence beside him. And just for tonight he would not think about what might happen when the two of them reached the valley and civilization. About what would happen if the people they met refused to believe that Troff was only a dog. There would be time enough to think of that later when other fears were less pressing.

Vague fears at first, that only drifted invisibly in the strange silence, but later, in the depths of the night, were transformed into dark shadows with great red eyes.

The cries came first, long pitiful wails that throbbed up and down the scale and then faded away to nothing. Then the silence returned and it was not until later, when the fire had burned low, and Tymmon had finally fallen asleep, that the dark shadows gathered.

Tymmon woke suddenly to the realization that Troff was on his feet and growling deep in his throat. Throwing back his blanket, he sat up and stared out into the surrounding darkness. And then he saw them, silhouetted against the starlit river. Shadows, strange humpbacked blobs of darkness that circled stealthily on silent feet.

With shaking hands Tymmon seized the dagger and waved it threateningly, but the shadowy circling continued without pause or change of pace. But then, realizing that the fire was very low, he dropped the weapon, in order to throw a log of firewood onto the glowing coals. Sparks flew upward and the shadows stopped pacing and turned to stare at him with great red eyes. For a moment he froze, unable to move hand or foot. Even his heart seemed to have stopped beating.

Only his racing mind seemed unaffected. "Demons," his mind told him. "They are demons from the depths of hell. Your breath has stopped and your heartbeat. They have turned you to stone."

But then his heart throbbed again with a great rib-shaking thud. He gasped for breath, and leaning forward, he added another log and then a handful of dead leaves to the fire.

The flames shot upward, Troff's growl broke out into a thunderous roar, and the shadows retreated back into the darkness.

"What are they?" Tymmon asked Troff. "What creatures are they?" But Troff's growling answer was not for him.

Stay away, the growl said. Stay away. There is no helpless prey here.

For another hour, or perhaps two, Troff sat stiffly, staring out into the darkness. Beside him, Tymmon also watched and waited, and kept the fire high and bright. The shadows did not return, but even so there was no more sleep that night. No sleep until, in the soft gray light of dawn, Troff yawned and stretched and said the danger was over. They both slept then, but it was not long before a hot bright sun cleared the hills beyond the river and, beating down fiercely upon them, forced them to awaken.

"What were they?" Tymmon asked again that morning as he made up his pack. "Were they demons, or perhaps wolves? Were they wolves, Troff?"

But Troff only growled and, looking fiercely toward the wooded hillside, said that he had chased them away. That he had chased them away and they would not return.

"I hope you are right," Tymmon said. "In any case I think we should not wait to fish again in this place. I think that we should leave as soon as possible."

And with his eyes still turned toward the hillside, Troff said that he agreed. When all was ready, Tymmon shouldered his pack and then, with the gargoyle trotting close beside him, began to wind his way southward through the boulder-strewn canyon.

They walked all that day, eating nothing but some half-ripe berries, a lizard, and a great ugly frog. It was Tymmon who found and ate the berries, and Troff who devoured all of the lizard as well as the frog, after Tymmon made it clear that he was not interested in sharing. Thus they were ravenously hungry and bone-achingly tired when, not long before sunset, they came out of a thick stand of young trees that grew along the bank of the river.

Ahead of them was an open stretch of grassland, and not far away a herd of oxen and cattle were grazing peacefully. Closer still, sitting on a tree stump, was a human being. The first human, other than the two brigands, that Tymmon had seen for many days. Grabbing Troff by the scruff of his neck, he pulled him to a stop and retreated back into the shelter of the saplings.

The cowherd, for such he seemed to be, was about Tymmon's size, and appeared to be almost as ragged and dirty. Completely unaware that he was being watched, he was whistling tunelessly to himself and whittling on a piece of wood.

"Look," Tymmon whispered. "A boy. The cowherd is only a boy. Remember now. You are a dog." He again grabbed Troff by the loose skin on the back of his neck and shook him. "Remember. A kindly, good-natured dog. Like this." Tymmon extended his tongue and panted, while with one arm he reached back to demonstrate the friendly waving of a tail. Troff watched with interest.

But then Tymmon's arm, the one that was representing a waving tail, suddenly made contact with the point of the Spanish dagger. Muttering a muffled exclamation of pain, he was rearranging the weapon in his belt, when he noticed the expression on Troff's face. His head cocked to one side, the gargoyle was grinning, in a familiar and particularly maddening way. In exactly the way that Lonfar had always smiled when some plan he had spoken against turned out badly.

"Troff," Tymmon was starting to say angrily when he suddenly realized that Troff was right. At least for the moment, he was entirely right to fear the dagger. It was, for the moment at least, dangerous. What would the cowherd, and other peasants as well, think if they saw the elegant and valuable weapon? Would they not, as Tymmon had done when he saw it in the possession of the brigand, be certain that it had been stolen from a murdered nobleman?

A few minutes later the dagger was hidden, along with

Komus's cap, at the bottom of Tymmon's pack. And Troff did indeed wave his tail in a convincingly doglike manner as they started out across the meadow to where the cow-herd was still busily carving his piece of wood. They were only a few feet away when he stopped whittling and, as if suddenly aware that he was not alone, quickly turned his head.

NINE

"**O**h, hello. Who be you . . ." the cowherd began and then, as he caught sight of Troff, "Holy saints protect me. Blessed Mary help me." Leaping behind the tree stump on which he had been sitting, he crouched down and, crossing himself feverishly, continued to beg for mercy. "Heavenly Father help me. Holy saints protect me."

Tymmon was talking, too, saying loudly and then more loudly, " 'Tis but a dog! A dog! He won't harm you. He is only a *dog*!"

He was beginning to think the cowherd was deaf, although certainly not mute, when the plea for heavenly help finally dwindled away into silence. Still cowering behind the tree stump so that only his head was visible, the boy looked from Tymmon to Troff and back again, his eyes jittery with fear and narrowed by suspicion.

"A dog?" he said at last, " 'Tis like no dog I ever seen. And who might you be, stranger?"

The voice was thin and quavery and tinged with the broad rolling accent of country folk. And the head, which from Tymmon's point of view seemed almost to be resting in a disembodied fashion on the tree stump, was narrow, pale-eyed, big-eared, and crowned with a dead-straw bristle of hair. Tymmon found himself grinning.

"My name is . . ." He paused, remembering that Tymmon, son of Komus, was a dangerous name to bear. But the hesitation was only for a fraction of a second while his racing mind considered and discarded several aliases, and then settled on Hylas—a name from one of Komus's tales of ancient times. "Hylas," he said. "I am Hylas, and my *dog* is called Troff. I am sorry that he startled you, but I am not entirely surprised. You see, he is from a rare breed raised only in the eastern countries and used there for the hunting of lions and griffins and other dangerous beasts. But he is quite tame and obedient. See how he will obey when I tell him to lie down and roll onto his back. Watch now.

"Lie down, Troff," he said. At the same time he held one hand at his side out of the boy's view, and wiggled the fingers in a scratching motion. And the gargoyle, as he always did at the very thought of a good scratch, flopped down and rolled belly-up. Tymmon knelt to give him a quick pat, and a brief and secret scratch. "See how well trained he is," he said as he regained his feet. "What is your name, friend? Tell me your name and I will make you known to him and tell him to do you no harm."

"I be called Char."

So Tymmon made a great show of telling Troff that this was Char, and that he was not to be harmed. And Troff rolled right side up and also made a great show of listening intently, as might an obedient dog. And when their act was over the cowherd came out from behind the stump.

Still watching warily, he began to edge toward where Troff was lying, grinning his white-fanged gargoyle smile. After several minutes of gradually increasing confidence, the peasant boy crouched down and touched Troff's head. He then smiled triumphantly at Tymmon, and went on touching, patting, and scratching with increasing enthusiasm. Troff's response was enthusiastic also. Watching the two of them, Tymmon began to feel uneasy. He had asked the silly beast to be friendly, not to make himself ridiculous fawning over the first simple-minded country bumpkin he happened to meet.

"Well," Tymmon said sharply, "we must be on our way. It is getting late and I had hoped to reach civilization before nightfall. Perhaps you could direct me to the nearest town or village."

"Late," the boy said suddenly, looking up toward the western sky. "Yes, it be late. I needs must hurry." He snatched up a long staff and started toward the grazing livestock.

Tymmon hurried after him. "The nearest village? Could you direct me?"

Already starting to wave his staff at his four-legged charges, the cowherd paused, and with his staff still raised, knit his brows in thought. After a remarkable amount of careful thought-taking he said slowly, "The nearest village? There be no village nearer than Bondgard." He nodded thoughtfully. "Yes. Bondgard be the nearest."

"And are you going to Bondgard?"

"Yes. I be."

"Excellent." Tymmon tried not to show his amusement. "Then it is to Bondgard that I would like to go. Would you permit my dog and me to accompany you?"

"You be wanting to go to Bondgard—with me?" the boy asked, and when Tymmon had made it clear that he was asking exactly that, he thought again and then said, "Well, come on then, for all of me. But I mustna tarry. If I be late my uncle will beat on me. He always beating on me when I be late." He started off again, waving his shepherd's staff, but within a moment he returned.

"That dog, there. Be he a stock harrier? My uncle says that all big dogs be harriers."

"A stock harrier? Oh, you mean a chaser of livestock. No, of course not. He is trained to chase only wild game." Tymmon's answer was quickly made, but as the shepherd began to gather the strayed cattle, he thought again. Troff was watching the rounding up of the livestock with an alarmingly alert and eager expression on his ugly face. Tymmon shrugged out of his pack, pulled out a length of rope, and formed one end into a loop. Then he approached cautiously, fearing that what he had in mind would not be easily accepted by such a mighty and untamed beast.

"Troff," he said uneasily, "this is a lead. Dogs are often kept on leads. Like this. See, this end goes around your neck and I hold the other. Thus dog and man cannot easily be separated. There. Is that not . . ."

Suddenly realizing that Troff seemed to be accepting the lead quite readily, Tymmon stopped babbling. He tugged gently on the rope, Troff followed, and within a few moments they were under way. Tymmon, with the now leashed Troff in hand, walked beside the cowherd, while up ahead the herd trotted and lumbered, six oxen, five milk cows, two gaunt and bony mules, three even scrawnier donkeys, and a half dozen goats.

As they made their way across the open pastureland and then down a long tree-bordered lane, Tymmon began to feel more confident. Things were going quite well. The cowherd no longer seemed to harbor any suspicions concerning Troff's true nature and Troff himself was behaving admirably. Not only had he been friendly to the peasant boy, but he also had accepted the lead, and had not, as Tymmon feared he might, mistaken the livestock for easy prey. And he now seemed to be content to trot along behind the herd at a discreet distance, as any well-trained farm dog might do. Gargoyles were, indeed, amazingly intelligent and adaptable creatures.

As they walked along, Tymmon decided to entertain his new friend as well as take his own mind off his painfully empty stomach. He would tell the boy the story of his life. The story, that is, of Hylas, who in the original tale, as told by Komus, was a young man of great beauty who lived in ancient Greece, but who Tymmon now reincarnated as the son of a brave huntsman who had been recently killed by brigands, forcing his son to go forth to seek his fortune.

"Where?" the cowherd asked.

"Where?" Tymmon asked. "Oh, you mean where did

we live? Oh, a great way from here. Far away to the south.
In a kingdom called . . ." Casting around in the remains
of old geography lessons he could find nothing suitable—
far away, but not so far as to be unbelievable. "Nordencor," he said at last, falling back on the distant kingdom
of his birth.

"Nor—den—cor!" Char pronounced the word with
some difficulty.

"Yes. Nordencor. My father served the lord of the castle, the lord Cyllo. My father was huntsman to Lord
Cyllo. He was a great hunter and a favorite with all the
nobility. But one day, only a few months since, when he
was out hawking with a small party, they were attacked by
a large band of brigands. My father fought with great
bravery and killed at least a dozen of the cutthroats single-
handedly, but at last he himself fell. And in gratitude the
lord Cyllo presented me with his favorite hunting dog—
Troff, here—and I set out to see the world."

As the story grew into an accounting of the hair-raising
adventures that Tymmon had experienced since leaving
home—some loosely based on fact and others purely fic-
tional—Tymmon became caught up in the telling. So
much so that for a time he almost forgot his empty stomach and the uncertainty of his situation. And as for Char,
he listened wide-eyed, so intent on Tymmon's story that
he often missed his footing and stumbled on the rutted
road. Even Troff, trotting alongside, seemed fascinated.
They were well into an especially thrilling account of an
attack by harpies when they reached the first outlying
cottages of the village of Bondgard, and Char was forced
to tear himself away to deliver a milk cow to its owner.

The cottager, a thin, pale man in rough peasant garb, stared at Tymmon and Troff curiously, but asked no questions and raised no outcry. The lead was helping, Tymmon thought, and thanked heaven for letting him think of it. A leashed animal, he told himself, is much more apt to be considered a dog, no matter what its size and appearance.

And it was indeed well that Troff was leashed, for as they made their way through the village, it became obvious that no Bondgard dog had ever borne even a slight resemblance to Troff. There seemed, in fact, to be very few dogs of any kind in the village. Tymmon had expected that Troff's presence would set off a riot of barking, but as they passed among the cottages only one dog appeared. One small, sharp-ribbed, scruffy animal who could easily have run beneath Troff's belly without so much as ducking its mangy head. Barking shrilly, he trotted out from behind a cottage, took one look at Troff, and scurried away, yelping in terror.

They met no other dogs, but farther on, as they crossed the churchyard square, some villagers came into view, two women at the well, another sweeping her doorstep, and two old men sitting on the church steps. They all stared at Troff, and the two women quickly moved to the far side of the well. But no one ran or shrieked, and one of the old men called out, "Hiya, boy. What's that creature you be leading there?" And Tymmon called back quickly and loudly, "A dog, sir. Only a big dog, bred for hunting."

Unlike the prosperous, thriving villages of Austerneve, this hamlet seemed to be a poor place. A number of cob and wattle cottages spread out in a patternless scatter from an unpaved market square occupied by a well, a muddy pond, and a small stone church with a broken-backed roof. As Char stopped at various dooryards to leave off his charges, Tymmon fell silent, wondering how he could find work or even charity in such a poverty-stricken community. When all the animals except for one cow had been delivered, Char, hurrying now, bade Tymmon good-bye.

"I be going to my uncle's now," he said. " 'Tis almost sunset. I be beaten if I be late."

"Wait, friend," Tymmon pleaded. "Before you go, could you tell me where I might find a place to spend the night? A place where I might be allowed to pay for my bed and a bite to eat by working. I am willing to do anything."

The boy stared at Tymmon for some time before he said, "Work. You want to work for food? I doan know about that. There be work in Bondgard town, but not much food, I think."

But Tymmon was too hungry to give up easily. "Your uncle?" he asked. "Would your uncle perhaps need another helper, even if only for a day or two? Could I at least ask him? He could do no more than say no."

At that Char shook his head doubtfully, but he made no further protest, and Tymmon followed him as he made his way on past the outskirts of the village to a slightly larger cob house that sat in the midst of several sheds and shacks in a cluttered and dirty farmyard. Char disappeared with the cow into one of the sheds, and left alone, Tymmon hesitated, trying to decide whether to approach the house. He was still standing near the cottage when a stoop-shouldered man with a sharp, anger-twisted face appeared in the doorway.

"Char," the man shouted and then noticing Tymmon, came toward him with long, swift strides. Then, as his gaze fastened on Troff, his pace slowed, and a few yards away he came to a stop.

"Who be you, and what be you doing in my dooryard?" he shouted. Tymmon had hardly begun to explain when he interrupted, bellowing, "Go! Begone with you. We have naught here for beggars and vagrants. Begone. And take that stock-killing beast with you."

Troff tugged on his leash, growling an angry threat, but when Tymmon pulled him away, he came. But he continued to look back over his shoulder and repeat the warning from time to time.

The sun was almost down when Tymmon and Troff returned to the center of the village. The square was deserted. Except for smoke that rose from a few chimney holes, the whole of Bondgard seemed as cold and lifeless as a deserted city. Perhaps a city of the dead, such as those that often figured in Mistress Mim's stories. Cities stripped of human life by the terrible sickness called the Black Death, or by the evil breath of dreadful creatures of the night. Lifting the collar of his cloak to cover his mouth and nose, Tymmon hurried across the square.

At the well he stopped long enough to drink briefly and then refill the dipper for Troff. But as the gargoyle drank, lapping up the water in great noisy gulps, Tymmon was suddenly overwhelmed by exhaustion and despair. Collapsing with his back against the well curbing, he buried his head in his arms. He was cold and exhausted and so terribly hungry that his stomach throbbed and burned with pain.

"What will we do?" he whispered. "What will we do?" He could feel Troff beside him, nosing and snuffling at his arms, but he kept his head down until he suddenly became aware of a new sound. "Hrrumphh," it went, as if someone was preparing his throat for speech. Then the sound repeated itself, Troff growled softly, and Tymmon quickly raised his head.

A few feet away a man was standing. An old man, and as Tymmon stared at him he saw that it was the old villager who had called to him from the church steps. Seen now at closer range it seemed he was very old indeed, his face deeply lined and his back bent and narrow. He stood leaning slightly forward, his gnarled and twisted hands resting on the top of a crooked walking stick.

"Boy," the man said, "what seek you here in Bondgard?"

Tymmon sniffled, caught his breath, and answered, "Work, sir. I seek work that I might feed myself and my dog. We are very hungry."

"You got no home to go to, boy?"

Tymmon began to tell the story of Hylas, son of the huntsman of Nordencor, but he had not gotten far when his voice failed him and he could only shake his head and say, "No, sir. I no longer have a home to go to."

The old man shook his head and, leaning heavily on his crooked staff, said, "There be many like you in these hard times. Bondgard be not a good place for the likes of you, boy. Nowadays the people here be too hungry theyselves to feel pain that others be starving. They be good people, mind you, but now they be too hungry to be kind. And even they that might feed a homeless child would not likely choose a boy like you. A lad who speaks with the accent of castle folk and owns a great, fine beast like yours, there. Bondgard dogs were scrawny creatures even in the good times, and now even most of them be long gone. Most of the Bondgard dogs be gone to the stewpot a long time since."

"Eaten," Tymmon said in horror. "The people of Bondgard ate their dogs?"

"The Bondgard folks eat whatever be left to them when all else be taken."

"Oh," Tymmon said, thinking that he now understood. "The brigands. Bondgard has been raided by the brigand companies?"

The old man shrugged and then shook his head. "No, not the brigand companies. Oh, they sneak a few goats or a cow now and then. But it be the lord of our castle and his knights who take our chickens and pigs and the grain from our harvests."

Tymmon stared at the old man. "The knights from your own castle. But knights are pledged to protect all who are weak and harmless, particularly those who live and work on their own lands."

"Oh, yes, they protect us, I suppose, from the lords and knights from other fiefdoms. And now and then they go into the forests a-chasing the brigands. But every year they raise up the taxes we be paying them for their protection, and then they come back again with more taxes to feed their guests for some great ceremony. Such like as the knighting of their sons, or the weddings of their daughters. I hear they be grand and glorious, the ceremonies of our noble lord, with folk from other castles coming from miles and miles around. But they be a great burden to us here in Bondgard."

The old man sighed deeply and then fell silent, and Tymmon was silent, too, thinking that the old man's story was much like the one Komus told about the noble knights who went forth to slay the dragon. And thinking, too, that there was no hope for him and for Troff in such a poor and starving village. At last he picked up his pack and turned to bid the old man good-bye.

"I thank you, sir, for your timely warning. I can see that it is useless for me to remain here."

"And which way will you be a-going?" the man asked.

"South. I will go to the south."

The old man nodded thoughtfully before he spoke. "Yes, it be well for you to go southward. There be the city called Montreff a few days' journey to the south. Montreff be a great walled city where there be merchants and craftsmen who might need a willing worker."

So Tymmon thanked the old man for his advice and was turning away when a thin old hand reached out to stop him.

"Wait, boy," the old man said, and digging into a leather pouch that hung at his belt, he pulled out a small loaf of bread and thrust it into Tymmon's hands. "Take it," he said, and when Tymmon tried to protest, he went on. "No, no. It be much too hard and stale for my weak old teeth. Take it and away with you."

Later that night, just as twilight faded into darkness, Tymmon and Troff came across a deserted farmyard where the remains of a tiny cottage sagged earthward under a broken roof. Finding a fairly dry spot in a corner, Tymmon opened his pack, spread his blanket, and then carefully cut the loaf of bread into two pieces. Troff's portion was gone in a moment, but Tymmon ate his very slowly. It was, as the kind old man had said, stale and hard, but it had been a long time since anything had tasted so rare and wonderful.

TEN

I t was midafternoon when Tymmon and
Troff came out of a narrow valley into a
broad plain and saw before them the
walled city of Montreff. Dark against a
bold blue sky, it sat like a crooked crown
on top of a sprawling range of hills, its steep stone walls
soaring up to end in an elaborate trimming of battlements, turrets, and towers. A winding road, starting on
the valley floor, led upward, twisting and turning like a
great snake.

Tymmon, who had never seen such a large city, stopped
and stared, gasping in amazement. "Look, Troff, look
there, ahead of us. The city of Montreff."

Troff glanced briefly with little show of interest, and
flopped down in the dust at the side of the road. Looking
up at Tymmon accusingly from the tops of his eyes, he

sighed deeply. He was tired, he said, and hungry, and they had walked much too far.

Tymmon regarded him pityingly. The gargoyle's feet and legs were caked with dirt, and his ribs stood out sharply beneath his gray-brown hide. "I know," Tymmon told him, "but we are almost there now. Come on. Just a little farther." He tugged gently on the lead, Troff struggled to his feet, and they plodded slowly on along the dusty road.

It had been several days—Tymmon had lost track of exactly how many—since they left the village of Bondgard. And in that time they had walked endlessly and eaten but little. Only an occasional scrap—a bit of wormy meat thrown out by a fellow traveler, some bread donated by a kindly village woman, and the one good meal which Tymmon had been able to earn by helping to build a farmer's stone fence. Not to mention, and it would be best not to mention to anyone, a fine fat chicken that Troff had somehow managed to acquire in the midst of a dark night when they were camped not far from a small village.

Tymmon had, of course, scolded him soundly and had at once broken camp and moved on. But he had taken the chicken with him, and some hours later, in the midst of a small woods, he and Troff had shared a delicious chicken dinner.

But on this last day they had eaten almost nothing, and for some hours Tymmon had been barely able to force himself to move one foot ahead of the other, and now it seemed to be hope alone that was giving him the strength to keep moving. Hope that the city on the hill would somehow provide him and Troff with food and rest and shelter.

On the last leg of the journey, up the steep winding road to the great gate, their pace slowed even more. Other travelers, hurrying to reach the gate, began to stream past them. Now and then someone, a priest riding a donkey, two gypsy children running behind their family's cart, a well-dressed gentleman on a fine strong mule, glanced curiously in their direction. But for the most part they were ignored, except at one point when a passing group of peasant women noticed Troff—and reacted only by pointing and giggling. Tymmon found himself glaring after them and saying under his breath, "Silly women. Too ignorant to recognize an enchanted creature when one appears before your very noses." A few minutes later, however, when he and Troff arrived at the great gate with its flanking guard towers, he was glad enough that they were able to pass by unrecognized and unnoticed.

Inside the high walls the city of Montreff, like a gigantic beehive, swarmed with close-packed activity. Narrow curving streets crossed and recrossed, winding between tall stone buildings in a crowded and confusing maze. Small shops of every description spilled their goods out through doors and windows, almost into the right of way. And watchful shopkeepers kept an eye out for thieves while they hawked their wares to the passing crowd.

And people were everywhere. Every kind of human being bumped elbows with every other—troops of running and shouting children, finely dressed members of the nobility in litters or on horseback, rugged peasants in homespun smocks and gaiters, some leading trains of heavily laden mules or donkeys, sober well-clad merchants and their proudly plump wives. And here and there a whining beggar, pale-faced, thin, and ragged.

As Tymmon made his way through the crowds he kept tight hold on the rope collar around Troff's neck, and tried to keep between him and the nearest passersby. But if he had feared what a gargoyle's reaction would be to such a pressing horde of humans, his worries appeared to be unfounded. Troff still plodded silently beside him, with low-hung head and drooping tail. Now and then his eyes lit up eagerly, once when a farmer's cart passed with a load of squawking chickens, and again at the sight of a pack of hounds led by a huntsman. But for the most part he seemed to take little interest in the hubbub around him.

From time to time Tymmon spoke to him, saying, "It's all right, Troff. They mean no harm." Or "I know, old friend. Too many people. But you are behaving very well." At other times, when someone pressed near looking at the gargoyle with curiosity or concern, he would pat Troff's head and say loudly, "Good dog, Troff. Stout fellow," as he had often heard the Austerneve kennel master speak to one of King Austern's hounds.

Sometimes when Tymmon spoke to him, Troff would roll his great sad eyes, but he said nothing, maintaining a doglike silence just as Tymmon had told him that he must.

As they wandered through the crowded streets, Tymmon kept his eyes open for an establishment that might have use of a willing worker. He stopped first at a butcher's, where the owner took one look at Troff and screamed at them to remove themselves immediately from his premises. He tried next at an inn, where the manager, a large man with a huge head covered by a bush of curly red hair, listened to him kindly enough and then said that his own five sons were more than enough to do all the work that needed to be done, and eat up all the profits as well, without taking on two more mouths to feed, "And one of them of truly prodigious size," he added, looking at Troff.

A silversmith came next, and then, in rapid succession, a baker (at whose shop the smell of fresh-baked bread so flooded Tymmon's mouth that he could scarcely speak), a shoemaker, a weaver, and a maker of pots and pans. Some sent them away loudly and angrily and some were kinder, but they were all firmly certain that a dirty, ragged, and hungry-eyed boy and an enormous dog could be of no use to them.

The sky was reddening at sunset when Tymmon and Troff came into the large open square in front of the cathedral. At the top of a wide flight of stairs the huge bronze doors stood open. A trickle of people were making their way up and down the stairs, penitents heading for or coming from the confessionals, or supplicants on their way to pray before the shrines of their favorite saints. At the edge of the wide entryway a group of beggars crouched: a filthy old man with a twisted leg, several ragged children, and two gypsy women with babies in their arms. Tymmon shrugged out of his pack, sat down on the bottom step, and pulled Troff down beside him. For a time he only watched. Watched the passing crowd, and most of all the beggars, wondering if he was close enough to starvation to stifle his pride and reach out as they were doing, begging in a high-pitched voice for alms for the poor.

As he watched, a bitter and painful smile twisted his lips and he leaned forward, burying his face in his arms. To be a beggar. He, the son of a wellborn man. Of a man who, in truth, had chosen to live as a lowly court jester, but who had been born into a noble family. And now he, who had scorned his father for choosing the life of clown and minstrel, was to be forced to sink to the most degrading station of all—that of a common beggar.

A raw and burning tightness gripped his throat and his eyes were beginning to flood when he became aware that Troff was on his feet and moving about. Tightening his hold on the lead, he raised his head to see that Troff was pawing at the pack that lay at their feet.

"What are you doing?" Tymmon's voice was angry. The anger was mostly at himself for his childish and useless tears, but Troff lowered his head and rolled his eyes guiltily. "There is no food in the pack," Tymmon went on in a gentler tone. "There is nothing there that is of any use . . ." He paused suddenly. After a moment's thought he himself turned to the pack and began to untie its bindings.

"Troff," he said eagerly, "you are right. Perhaps there is something here that might be of use—if we could sell it. Something that we could sell for enough to buy at least a bit of bread."

There was, of course, the Spanish dagger. That would bring by far the most, but it also might bring suspicion and even worse. What if the buyer accused Tymmon of stealing—as well he might, since a dirty, ragged boy could not have come by such an expensive object legally. No. It would have to be something else.

Not the dagger. And no, not the cap. He could not sell Komus's cap. And besides, who would want to buy such a thing? That left the tinderbox, the knife, the ax and—the flute. The flute. Of all his meager possessions the flute was perhaps the least necessary.

Taking the old flute, so beautifully carved of dark satiny wood, out of the pack, Tymmon held it in both hands, running his fingers along its familiar surface. He could not recall exactly when his father had given it to him, he had been so young at the time. But he remembered well how proud and delighted he had been when, as a child of four or five, he had several times been allowed to entertain the king's noble guests by his playing. How he had played at the wedding banquet when the king's son, Prince Mindor, had married the lady Hanna, at the christening of their baby daughter, and at other grand celebrations. He could even remember some of the tunes he had played. Slowly, lost in memory, Tymmon raised the flute to his lips and began to play.

It was a slow tune that he had chosen. Sweet but sad, and there was a recurring refrain that clung in the mind, bringing with it a soft and yearning melancholy. Tymmon let the music flow out from his heart and closed his eyes against the tears that arose again, this time from the music's bittersweet lament. He played the song through to the end and began again, but when he came to the refrain, the sweet, low notes of the flute were joined by another, wilder and more discordant, sound. As he had so often done in the forest, Troff was singing along with the music.

Somehow Troff's singing made the threat of tears even greater, and Tymmon was forced to keep his eyes shut as he went through the song again. And again at each repetition of the refrain, Troff joined in. When the last note of the second playing drifted away to silence, there was another sound. A murmuring that came from very nearby. And when Tymmon opened his eyes he saw that he and Troff were surrounded by a small group of people, two noble ladies with their maids and attendants, and a tall old man dressed in a long, dark robe. As Tymmon stared in astonishment the murmur grew, one of the ladies began to clap her hands, and soon the others were clapping also.

"Bravo, lad," the tall man said. "You are a gifted musician. And your large companion here is obviously gifted too."

For a moment Tymmon was too astounded to do more than blurt out a stammering "Thank you, sir." But when the lady who had begun the clapping asked for another tune, "Perhaps something more cheerful this time?" his mind regained its usual keenness.

"Gladly, my lady," he said, and lifting the flute, he began another tune, a lively, high-pitched melody. One that, in the past, had brought a quick response from Troff. And Troff did sing again, this time in short, sharp bursts, quite unlike his earlier mournful wailing. And while he played, Tymmon watched his audience with growing excitement.

The tall old man listened smilingly and the ladies and

their attendants seemed delighted, the ladies covering their smiles daintily, while two or three of the maids were almost collapsing in fits of giggling laughter. Before the piece was ended others had joined the group of listeners, and a sizable crowd had begun to form around the ragged boy and the great scruffy beast at the foot of the cathedral steps. As Tymmon went on playing, the crowd continued to laugh and clap, and many of them, as they went away, dropped a coin or two onto the cobblestones near Tymmon's feet.

It was only a little more than an hour later when, after stopping to do some very important shopping, Tymmon and Troff arrived back at the inn where the red-haired manager had turned them away in a kindly manner. But this time they came only to ask for a place to sleep. They found the innkeeper presiding over the large common room of the inn.

"I have money now," Tymmon said quickly at the large man's questioning frown.

"And where did you get this money, lad?" The innkeeper's tone was still kindly but his eyes had narrowed suspiciously. "I will have no thieves spending the night in my inn."

"No, no," Tymmon said. "Troff and I—Troff is my dog here—Troff and I earned the money by playing the flute—and singing."

The red-haired man's eyes narrowed further. "You and your dog played the flute—and sang?"

Tymmon glanced around the room. A few travelers were eating at the long tables before the enormous hearth, and three or four others stood around the fireplace, tankards in hand. "I will show you, sir. If you will allow me?"

The innkeeper's frown turned into a reluctant grin. "This I will have to see," he said. "But come with me out into the courtyard. I would not want this demonstration to disturb my guests."

So Tymmon played again and Troff sang in the now darkening courtyard, lit only by the two large torches that illuminated the inn's entrance. And when they had finished, the red-haired innkeeper laughed so hard that his huge belly bounced up and down.

Then he slapped Tymmon on the back. "Well, well, lad," he said, "in God's truth I took you to be a liar and a thief, and I see now that you are not the first and probably not the second. So I must ask your pardon, and if I had a spare bed I would indeed offer it to you for some of your honestly earned money. But as you must have seen, the town is full of holiday visitors and there is not a—" He paused and then went on, "Unless you would not mind a night in the stable. There is a cot in the harness room that was once used by a stableboy. 'Tis not much, but it would be better, I think, than a night on the streets among the pickpockets and beggars. Would you not agree?"

Tymmon agreed as quickly and heartily as he was able. The innkeeper went back to his guests, and a moment later one of his equally red-haired sons appeared and directed Tymmon to his new lodgings.

The room was small and smelled mustily of horses and sweated leather. It contained only a wooden bench and a bed that was scarcely more than a wider bench, but on that night it seemed better than any palace bedchamber. As soon as the door had closed behind them, Tymmon untied his pack and brought out the purchases he had made from the street vendors in the cathedral square. There was a candle, two large meat pies, a sausage, some dried fruit, and a large loaf of bread.

After lighting the candle, Tymmon placed it on the bench, and arranged the food around it. He took a brief moment to offer thanks to God for such a marvelous feast, and then the eating began. And when it was finally finished, his stomach—and no doubt Troff's also—ached pleasantly from overstretching.

The last crumb had hardly disappeared when Troff was asleep, sprawled on his side on the hay-strewn floor. Tymmon spread his blanket on the thin pallet, stretched out, and closed his eyes, but for him sleep was not so easily come by. Although his body was very tired, his mind seemed to be full of newfound energy. Calling up again and again the adventures of the day, it leaped and skittered and jiggled excitedly from one thing to the other and back again.

First and most often it dwelt on what had happened on the cathedral steps. He had, it seemed, suddenly and without aforethought, stumbled upon a way to keep himself and Troff from starving. He could stay alive by becoming a kind of jongleur, one of the many lesser musicians who made their livelihood by accompanying well-known singers or troubadours. Only in his case the troubadour was something less—or more—than human.

It was not, he told himself, a high calling. It was not a profession of which one might be proud. Especially not one who had scorned his father's means of earning a livelihood as demeaning and shameful. His father who, after all, was not only a clown but also wrote the words and music for his own songs just as did the troubadours, many of whom were held in high regard. And now he, Tymmon, would be a street musician, playing for coppers tossed by passersby.

No, it was not a thing to rejoice over—that was for certain. But the mystery was that he knew he was rejoicing. When he went back in memory to the cathedral steps and the surrounding throng, again and again his heart sang with delight. And it was not just that the awful fear of starvation had been lifted. No, there was more to it than that. What it was exactly was hard to understand, but he knew it had to do with delighted smiles and laughter and the clapping of many hands. Tymmon smiled into the near darkness and told himself that he would think on it more in the morning.

On the floor beside the pallet Troff stirred and mumbled in his sleep, and Tymmon reached down to pat the great round head. It was Troff's doing, he told himself. He would never have thought of it by himself. It was Troff who had advised him to open the pack and see what was there that could be of use. Not in words, perhaps. Not even, this time, in the unspoken words with which he often communicated. But when he had pawed at the pack the message had surely been there.

"You are a true friend," Tymmon whispered. "And a wise and clever one too. You called my attention to the flute without speaking, or behaving in any way that might have given away your true nature."

Troff sighed heavily, raised his head, and looked at Tymmon questioningly.

"Your true nature as an enchanted beast," Tymmon explained, and Troff sighed again and went back to sleep.

It was true. All day long Troff had behaved in a very doglike manner. Closing his eyes, Tymmon could picture him as he plodded along, as would an obedient dog at his master's side. And he had looked as well as acted very doglike. The picture that had risen before Tymmon's eyes was indeed that of a great dog. Bigger than most, certainly, and uglier, with a face most unlike any dog that Tymmon had ever seen. But in many other ways, quite like a dog.

The thought suddenly made Tymmon uneasy. He opened his mouth to ask Troff, as he had asked before, if he were truly a gargoyle, but he was stopped by the sound of deep, even breathing. It was not fair to awaken him again when he was so tired. Instead Tymmon closed his eyes and brought back another image. A picture this time of Troff as he had appeared across the fire on that first night in the Sombrous Forest. On that night when no one could have doubted for a moment that he was, indeed, an enchanted beast—a living gargoyle.

Tymmon sighed and yawned, and as he drifted toward sleep a new understanding came to him. An understanding vague and indistinct, but full of a comforting certainty. Of course, Troff was seen as a dog when he wanted to be. An enchanted creature could surely enchant the eyes of the beholder so that they would see him as he wanted to be seen.

Tomorrow I'll think more on that also, he told himself before he blew out the candle and fell into a long, deep sleep.

ELEVEN

On that first morning in Montreff, Tymmon awoke to a mind-shattering clamor. The sound came from everywhere and filled every space so deeply that it almost seemed to arise from inside his skull or even from the pit of his stomach. Tymmon's sleep-dulled mind, accustomed to the silence of forest mornings, was momentarily stunned and bewildered. And then he remembered—and understood.

The clanging, ringing, chiming waves of sound were only the bells of many churches, announcing Sunday morning and the hour of prime. Leaping up from his pallet, Tymmon stumbled over Troff, caught himself, and hurried to the door, a door that opened onto a stableyard at the rear of the White Boar Inn in the city of Montreff.

The sun had not yet risen above the horizon, but a clear pale sky shimmered with its reflected light. An unpaved and dusty courtyard lay before him, beyond which rose the rear wall of the inn, half timbered and three stories high. On his right the stables, long and low and roughly thatched, bordered the courtyard on one side. And directly before him in the center of the yard was a covered well, surrounded by troughs and basins and a jumble of upended pails and tubs.

When the bells ceased to ring, the silence of early dawn returned except for, from somewhere nearby, a lonely rooster's morning challenge. Up on the second and third stories of the inn the windows were still shuttered against the light. No one stirred in the courtyard. The patrons of the White Boar, it seemed, enjoyed their Sunday morning slumber.

Tymmon stretched and breathed deeply, savoring the almost forgotten smells of civilization—musty, spicy, smoky odors so unlike those of the forest. The deep breath ended in a shivery gasp, as a tingle of nervous excitement raced up his spine. What would Dame Fortune have in store for him today in the great city of Montreff? He could not even imagine. Glancing down at his dirty and bedraggled self, he came to the quick decision that it would be better to meet whatever fate had in store in a cleaner and more presentable condition.

A few minutes later, with the aid of a pail of water from the well, some vigorous splashing and scrubbing, and the spare jerkin from his pack (a little cleaner and less tattered than the other), he was ready to go. Shouldering his pack, he picked up Troff's leash.

"Well, Troff," he said. "Shall we try our luck again as minstrels?"

Troff, who had been patiently watching Tymmon's preparations from a spot near the door, leaped to his feet, saying that he was indeed ready and had been for some time.

Tymmon grinned as Troff bounced around him, but then, as he slipped the collar over the gargoyle's head, he frowned and spoke sternly. "Remember. Remember not to speak to anyone but me and then only silently. Your behavior must at all times be that of an ordinary dog."

Troff had stopped leaping and stared questioningly at Tymmon, his head cocked.

Tymmon nodded. "Yes," he said. "I know. Except for the singing." He grinned. "Your behavior must be that of an ordinary singing dog."

A few moments later, as they were crossing the courtyard, a voice called "Good morning," and Tymmon turned to see Master Harcor, the innkeeper, standing in the kitchen entryway. He wore an apron over a well-made jerkin and doublet, his boots were clean and new, and his red hair gleamed in the early sun. "Good morning," he called again, and as Tymmon approached, "It would seem that you slept well last night. At least your complexion has a far healthier hue this morning."

Tymmon grinned and touched his face. " 'Tis the color of food and rest, sir. And cleanliness. 'Tis the true color of my skin, actually, recently relieved of several layers of dirt. I took the liberty of making use of some water from your well."

"So I had guessed." Harcor grinned. "And judging by the change in your appearance, I would say that water from my well has seldom been put to better use. Are you off, then, on further journeys?"

"Oh, no, sir. At least not immediately. I would like to stay here in Montreff for several days, at least. And I would like very much to continue to rent your harness room at the same daily rate, if I may."

The innkeeper shrugged. "I see no reason to refuse," he said. "As long as your great beast here does not frighten my guests or their horses." His eyes narrowed, and for a moment he contemplated both Tymmon and Troff thoughtfully. "Tell me, lad. Did you say you were from . . . ?"

Tymmon could not remember giving the innkeeper that information but he said quickly, "Nordencor. I am called Hylas, son of Lindor, and I am from the fiefdom of Nordencor."

"I see. And you were there born and raised? And to what station in life?"

Tymmon looked up quickly, a faint alarm sounding in the back of his mind.

The innkeeper smiled disarmingly. "I ask only because your knowledge of music seems unusual for one of your apparent station. And there is also your manner of speech. Your tongue seems trained to the accents of court and castle. And as innkeeper I have dealings with people of all ranks and stations and I have learned to recognize the accents of different regions as well as those common to people from different walks of life."

So Tymmon again told his story of being the son of the unfortunate huntsman of Nordencor. He made the part concerning his father's death even more heroic, and went on to explain how, living with his father in the lord's castle, he had sometimes played with the children of the nobility and thus had perhaps, without intending to, picked up some of their habits of speech.

"I see," Harcor said with what seemed to be sympathetic understanding. " 'Tis a sad tale and a most sad fate to be alone and homeless at such a tender age." His words were kindly, but his still-narrowed eyes and tilted eyebrows were perhaps saying something else.

Later, as Tymmon, with Troff beside him, made his way along the narrow streets of Montreff among a scattering of early-rising citizens, his mind returned to Harcor and his searching questions. Did the innkeeper's probing arise from simple curiosity? Or had he heard of a reward offered for the capture of a young fugitive?

"What do you think, Troff?" Tymmon said. "Do you think he knows who I really am?"

Troff cocked his head and seemed about to answer when Tymmon noticed a passerby's amused interest. Stooping quickly, he pretended to be adjusting Troff's collar while he whispered in his ear, "Remember, Troff. Do not answer." Then he hurried on, telling himself silently that he must remember in the future not to speak to Troff in public, except in the manner that one speaks to a dog.

Even at that early hour on Sunday morning the cathedral square was filling rapidly with churchgoers. Men, women, and children, of every class and dressed in everything from rough homespun to the finest velvets and satins, were making their way to and from the cathedral.

At the bottom of the wide stairway Tymmon stopped

and looked around at the passing throng. He found that he was breathing deeply, and a rapid pulse was beating at the base of his throat. But it was a condition that did not seem to be caused by fright. Or at least not entirely by fright. There was also an element of anticipation that was, if not entirely pleasant, at least certainly exciting.

He looked down at Troff. The gargoyle was sitting beside him, surveying the crowd with calm interest. Tymmon took a deep breath, pulled the flute from the pack, and raised it to his lips. "Ready?" he whispered to Troff. "Are you ready to sing?"

Tymmon was barely into the first song when a merchant and his family stopped to listen. They crowded around him, a short man with a tall wife, both well dressed and portly, and a horde of children, ranging in age from infancy to almost adult. A group of peasants, mostly women and children, came next, followed by a trio of richly clad young men. As Troff began his first refrain there were startled gasps, much laughter, and then, as the song ended, a burst of applause. Others joined the crowd and soon coins began to be tossed onto the cobblestones.

During the second song, the lively chansonette, there were excited gasps from the children, and when it was over the merchant gave generously as each of his children demanded a copper to personally place in front of Troff. One by one they crept forward and dropped their coin, each of them trying to place it closer to Troff's feet, the younger ones then scurrying back shrieking with delighted fear.

Tymmon had just begun a second slow tune, and Troff was in the midst of his mournful lament, when a stern voice cried, "Stop. In the name of all that is holy, stop this unseemly howling immediately."

The people fell silent as a dark-robed priest pushed his way among them. Seizing Tymmon by the collar, he had started to shake him, when a very different sound from Troff caused him to release his hold and retreat up the stairs so quickly that he tripped on the skirt of his vestments and almost fell.

"Stop at once," he cried from a safer distance, and then, turning to the listeners, he began to berate them for wasting their time listening to worldly songs in such a sacred place on God's holy day. And also for wasting their money on an ungodly exhibition instead of saving it to buy candles or for other righteous purposes. Before the priest had ceased to speak, Tymmon had gathered up his earnings and, squeezing through the crowd, made his way quickly out of the square.

They tried their songs next in a smaller square, which seemed to be used as an outdoor market. The listeners were again numerous and enthusiastic, particularly the children, but the people here were mostly peasants and laborers and money was obviously scarce. When Tymmon prepared to leave sometime later, he found on the cobblestones only a few coppers, two green apples, and a half a loaf of bread.

During the remainder of the day they performed in various places with varying success. They also stopped a number of times to buy food and eat, and in their stable room that night they ate again as Tymmon counted their collection of coins and made plans for the future.

"If we are going to stay much longer in Montreff we

need to broaden our repertoire," he told Troff. "Some new songs perhaps? What do you think?"

Troff, who was nibbling at a flea on his rear leg, rolled his eyes at Tymmon and sighed.

"I know," Tymmon said. "You are tired of singing. You did not complain, but at the end of the day I could tell that you were loath to continue. And to sing so many times a day must indeed be hard on your throat. Perhaps we could add some other types of entertainment to our exhibition. When I was very young I often practiced tumbling and juggling with my father, and at one time I could play the rebec and the lyre as well as the flute. I stopped practicing some time ago but I think the skills would return quickly."

He glanced at his small store of coins. "Perhaps," he began, and then noticed that Troff was nearly asleep. "Well, I will think on it, and tomorrow we will speak of it some more."

That very night Tymmon laid many plans, and in the days that followed most of his ideas were turned into realities. He was soon able to purchase a rebec, a fine instrument with a graceful pear-shaped body and well-mounted strings. And his fingers soon regained enough of their old skills for him to be able to play the accompaniment as he sang a number of songs—many old folk songs and ballads, as well as many of the songs composed by his father. His voice, not yet deepened by approaching manhood, was clear and true, and his singing often earned as much applause as did Troff's, although much less laughter. Now and then he told one of his father's stories, complete with dramatic pantomime, and it was not long before his juggling and tumbling had improved enough so that he was able to include a brief demonstration of physical dexterity during each exhibition.

And Troff's role was expanding too. With only a few training sessions Tymmon had been able to teach him to perform a deep bow at the end of each presentation, and then to circulate through the crowd carrying a small pail in his mouth. Troff seemed to particularly enjoy that part of his performance, and he soon added his own special touches, stopping in front of listeners who had not yet contributed to regard them with an accusing stare—a tactic that always set the crowd to laughing and the penny-pincher to digging into his purse.

So Troff's part in their daily exhibitions grew, and to Tymmon's great relief, no one seemed to see him as anything magical or supernatural. Unlike the situation in the small villages where some people had certainly feared him as a monster, here in the city he seemed to be easily accepted as a dog. There had been, in fact, one man, an ancient pilgrim, who had spoken of seeing others of his breed in cities and castles in the low countries, where they were used in hunting as well as to pull small carts on the city streets.

Tymmon had suppressed a smile. It did not seem likely that gargoyles were being used as beasts of burden in the low countries. But Tymmon had not contradicted the pilgrim, since he was old and weak of eye and mind. And also, of course, because it was necessary that everyone should continue to see Troff as a dog.

It was only when they were alone at night in their small room in the stable that Troff was free to be his real self.

To transform himself into a mysterious and magical presence in the dim twilight, grinning his gargoyle grin, and sharing with Tymmon the thoughts of his gargoyle mind.

Before long their days had settled into a routine. Mornings at the cathedral square, except on Sundays and holy days, and then a round of shorter stops at several other squares and crossroads. By early afternoon a return to the inn for rest and rehearsals, and then another briefer visit to the central square between vespers and sundown.

Some audiences were more enthusiastic than others and more generous, and there were days when Tymmon's hoard of coins grew but little. But there was always enough to eat, a secure—if a bit chilly and flea-ridden—place to spend the night, and even more important, that rush of strange and unexplainable delight when hands clapped and faces lit with laughter.

To Tymmon's surprise, that mysterious joy did not fade away as time passed. Instead it seemed to grow as he became more sure of his ability to brighten dull eyes and set tired faces to smiling. Once or twice it occurred to him to wonder if his father had felt the same when he performed in King Austern's court, and if he, too, had thrilled to the sudden joy in sorrowful eyes. If, for instance, there had been a time when Komus's clowning had first brought a smile back to the face of the old king, after the terrible death of his only son, the brave and handsome Prince Mindor. Surely there had been such a time and now Tymmon knew how Komus had felt at that moment.

So Tymmon's life as a jongleur and minstrel continued to flourish, and at the White Boar all seemed well also. Harcor and two or three of his many sons still seemed to show a deep and searching interest in Tymmon and his background, but no one had mentioned Austerneve or a reward offered for the capture of a fugitive. Nor had they tried to restrict his movements in any way.

One day, after Tymmon had greatly improved his appearance with a haircut and some new articles of clothing, the innkeeper asked him if he would like to trade a few songs for an evening meal. And from that day on when the sun had set and the common room of the inn was full of ale drinkers and travelers, Tymmon and Troff played and sang. And when the performance was over they sat before the hearth in the enormous kitchen and ate roasted meats, rich stews and soups, sweet pastries, and many other wonderful things.

It was, compared to the hard, cold, hungry days in the forest, a good life. Not, of course, anything like the wonderful existence, full of fame and honor and high adventure, of a young man born into a noble family, but better than . . . Better than life in the forest, where one was threatened daily by harpies and brigands and starvation.

And, it sometimes occurred to him, certainly better than that of villagers such as Char, the poor mistreated cowherd. And better than that of all the people of the village of Bondgard, taxed into starvation by their greedy lord.

And probably better than—but he tried not to think of that. Tried not to wonder where Komus was and what sort of life he was now living. But he did think of his father—over and over and over again until he grew angry at himself and, as he had often done in the past, at Komus also.

At Komus for so senselessly giving up his homeland and heritage to flee to Austerneve and become a court jester. And for something else too. For taking foolish risks that Tymmon had only started to understand since he had begun again to sing Komus's songs and tell his stories.

For now that he was older and was once again learning and rehearsing the things that Komus had written, it was becoming clear to him that his father had included in his performances criticisms of powerful people and institutions—more or less subtly sarcastic comments on the behavior of the high and mighty of both church and castle. On crusaders who plundered farms and villages on their way to the Holy Land, and priests of the church who became wealthy selling pardons and relics. And of highborn lords who pretended friendship while plotting evilly against their friends and neighbors.

There were songs that Tymmon had once thought simply amusing, which he now saw as having a deeper meaning. He had watched some peasants laughing bitterly and a little uneasily as he sang a song about greedy landlords. And he had seen a group of students chuckling over the verses about the churchman who swore an oath of poverty every morning before he went out selling pardons to poor ignorant peasants. And as he sang Komus's songs and told his stories, it occurred to Tymmon to wonder if Black Helmet could have been someone who felt he had been mocked.

Black Helmet. He still could not even guess who the great thick-bodied knight in the strange dark armor could have been. But it was beginning to be apparent that

Komus, whom Tymmon had once thought to be naught but a harmless clown, might have had dangerous enemies. Komus must have known that to ridicule such things and people could be hazardous. Why did he continue to take the risk—to his own life and safety, and that of his son also? It was a question that Tymmon asked himself many times, but only during the dark and silent hours before dawn. At other times, in the rush and press of life in the great walled city of Montreff, it was not too difficult to keep his mind on other things.

Days passed. Spring was warming into summer and berries and fine fresh vegetables were appearing on the peddlers' tables in the market square. At the White Boar Inn business was good as more citizens took advantage of the better weather to travel on business or pilgrimage. And every night Tymmon and Troff performed to larger and larger crowds.

It was on one night in early May, when the audience had been particularly large and enthusiastic, that an old man approached Tymmon as the performance ended. He was curiously dressed in a shabby velvet tunic patterned in red and black, and on his long thin legs were dirty purple gaiters with elaborate tasseled lacings. His stringy hair and pointed beard were almost white, but his eyes, under shaggy brows, were a sharp, keen blue.

"You are greatly gifted, lad," he said, with a gap-toothed grin. "And your dog is a priceless treasure."

"Thank you, sir." Tymmon slung his rebec over his shoulder and picked up the flute. "My dog and I both thank you for your kind remarks."

The man smiled and nodded and went on standing

where he blocked the passageway from the crowded room. Putting his hand on Tymmon's shoulder he leaned forward and, in a harsh whisper, said, "Would you join me yonder where the crowd is less pressing? I would like to speak further with you."

Tymmon hesitated. Food was waiting in the kitchen, and besides there was something in the intensity of the old man's stare that made him uneasy. "You are most kind, sir," and then, as he bent to pick up Troff's leash, "but at the moment . . ."

The grip on Tymmon's shoulder tightened. "I, too, have been a minstrel," the old man said. And then as Tymmon straightened he bent closer, and staring with searching, narrowed eyes, he added, "And I, too, am from Nordencor."

TWELVE

A s the man from Nordencor led the way across the crowded common room, other guests smiled and nodded at Tymmon, and a fat-faced merchant in a long surcoat trimmed with fur reached out to press a coin into his hand. But he barely acknowledged their smiles or even their coins. His mind was too busy elsewhere, asking frightening questions. Questions that might well have even more frightening answers.

"Who . . ." he began once, and again, "How did you know . . ." but the stranger only shook his head and said, "Wait. Wait."

It was not until they were seated on a bench in a dark alcove that he leaned forward, grasped Tymmon's hand, and with his scraggly beard quivering, said, "Let me introduce myself. I am called Jarn. I am a traveling jongleur now, but I was once a minstrel and a tutor of music in the

court of Lord Cyllo of Nordencor. And you, I understand, are called Hylas—from the same city. Is that correct?"

"How did you know?" Tymmon asked. "Who told you
that I was from Nordencor?"

"Why, Master Harcor, our red-haired host, told me."

"I see," Tymmon said. And he did see—but only in
part. What he saw was that the old man had learned that
Tymmon—or Hylas, the son of Lindor—claimed to be a
native of his own city. And since he obviously had not
heard of any such person, nor of a huntsman named
Lindor who had recently died a tragic death, he possibly
knew that Tymmon had lied about his parentage. But
what Tymmon did not understand was why he had bothered to inquire in the first place. Unless . . . unless he
knew of the reward offered by Black Helmet and suspected that Tymmon was, in reality, from Austerneve and
the fugitive son of Komus, the court jester.

"Why did you want to know my birthplace?" he asked,
and even before the old minstrel began to answer he felt a
strange premonition that the answer would be something
of deep and lasting importance. As he waited he was suddenly chilled by a wave of fear, and felt an almost irresist-
ible urge to cover his ears with his hands and run away.

For a long moment there was no answer as the old man
only sat staring searchingly into Tymmon's face, but then
he began to speak. "It has been some years since I left
Nordencor to make my living as a traveling jongleur. But
before that time I lived most of my life in that city, entertaining in the lord's court and in the homes of the nobil-

ity, and instructing those who wished to learn the art of
singing and playing music."

He stopped suddenly, and taking Tymmon's chin in his
hand, he turned his face from one side to another. "Yes,
yes," he murmured. "It is remarkable. But according to
our host you are the son of a huntsman. It is, indeed,
remarkable." He then seemed to fall into a deep reverie
from which he did not arouse himself until Tymmon
reached out and touched his arm.

"Sir. What is it? What is remarkable?"

"Yes. Yes. It is the resemblance. The resemblance is
remarkable. You see, I had, during those years, one student who came to me to learn the art of song as well as
that of playing on various musical instruments. He was,
when the lessons began, only a child. No more than seven
or eight years of age. He was a comely child and greatly
gifted in many ways, and he loved music dearly. He continued to study with me and to practice even after he
began his training for the knighthood."

Tymmon, who had already guessed who this gifted student must have been, caught his breath. It was true, then.
His father had come from a noble family and had even
trained for the knighthood. He had never really doubted
—since he had never known Komus to lie to him—but it
was so hard to believe that anyone could choose to throw
away such a birthright.

"What was he called?" he demanded. "What was the
name of your student?"

"He was called Lucan. Lucan, son of the lord Tymmoor." Jarn paused and looked sharply at Tymmon.
"Have you then heard of such a person?"

Tymmon shook his head. "No," he said. "Not by that name. What did he look like, this Lucan?"

Jarn smiled wryly. "Much as you do, lad. That is why I asked the landlord about your background. Oh, he was of a lighter complexion, with hair of a light golden brown, but in all other aspects he looked very much as you do. But it was not just appearance that led me to wonder about your parentage. It is your gift also. One does not forget easily a voice so sweet and true. And with such similar tricks of tone and voicing. It was just so that Lucan, son of Tymmoor, sang for me when he was a boy of your age."

Tymmon found his hands were trembling and he gripped them together and pressed them between his knees. Taking a deep, wavering breath, he asked, "And what happened to him—your student? Why did he leave Nordencor?"

Jarn's eyes narrowed. "Aha," he said. "You know then that he left the city? What else do you know concerning Lucan, son of Tymmoor?"

Tymmon shook his head wildly. "Nothing. Nothing of anyone by that name. But I think . . ."

He paused and Jarn nodded. "I see. But by another name perhaps? Yes. Yes, I see why that would be."

"Why? Tell me why. Why did he leave Nordencor and change his name and . . ."

It was some time before Jarn spoke again. "I see that you do not know. And I am, indeed, loath to be the one to tell you. But having gone this far . . ." There was another pause and then he continued. "It was soon after his knighting that Lucan was married. His bride was a lovely maiden, Lianne she was called, the daughter of Lord Aylion, the ruler of a small neighboring fiefdom. They had been married only a few years and I believe there had been a child. Yes, there was. A boy it was. A child who would now be . . . perhaps . . ." He stared at Tymmon with narrowed eyes. "Of perhaps a dozen years of age."

"Thirteen," Tymmon said briefly.

"Yes, thirteen." Jarn smiled. "It was when this child was still little more than a babe in arms that Lucan was ordered by Lord Cyllo of Nordencor and the lord bishop to take part in a crusade against an uprising of heretics. And it was while he was gone that his young wife . . . died."

Tymmon nodded. "Of a fever?"

Jarn paused again, this time for so long and meanwhile staring in such a strange fashion that Tymmon became more and more uneasy. "No," the old minstrel said at last. "Not of a fever. You see, your mother—that is, the bride of Lucan—was accused of witchcraft, and while he was in the south with the lord's army she was—executed as a witch."

Executed as a witch. Burned at the stake. His mother. The words seemed at first to have no meaning—or none that Tymmon could grasp. And when his mind did begin to function, some of its shock and horror must have reached Troff, who suddenly rose from where he had been sprawled at Tymmon's feet and, staring at the old man, began to growl softly.

"No, Troff. It's all right," Tymmon said at last. But the gargoyle was not easily convinced, and it was some time before he backed away. And even then he remained sitting with his eyes rolling anxiously between Tymmon's face and that of the old man.

"Why?" Tymmon at last managed to ask. "Why was she accused of witchcraft?"

The jongleur shook his head and went on shaking it for so long that Tymmon began to fear that he did not intend to answer. But at last he said, "Why? It is hard to say why such things happen. There had been bad times in Nordencor. Drought and famine and much illness, and there were those who felt the need to lay the blame for all the misfortune on some evil force. A great fear of witches had grown up throughout the countryside. I am not sure why Lucan's lady was singled out except that she was—had always been—different. Beautiful and intelligent and gifted in all the arts—she too was one of my students for a time—but unlike the other maidens in many ways."

He paused again and his eyes went dim and blurred with old memories. "There had always been rumors. She was the only child of parents who were in their middle years when she was born—and her hair and eyes were dark while her parents were of fair complexion. Some whispered that she had gypsy blood, although her parents swore that she was born to them and was their true and only heir. And she had lived much of her childhood at her father's manor in the hill country, where some said she had been allowed to roam through the woods and fields like a wild thing, playing with birds and animals, and . . ."

"And talking to them. It was she who talked to animals."

"What did you say, lad?"

Tymmon had not known that he had spoken aloud, but it seemed that Jarn had heard him. "Nothing," he said quickly. "And my fath—and the knight Lucan? Was he too accused of witchcraft?"

"No. No, I do not think so. But soon after he returned to Nordencor and learned of his wife's death, he disappeared, and the child with him. No one knew what had become of them. But there were some who said that he had been behaving wildly. Threatening people in high places and making accusations. Against his wife's cousin, who had friends in court and church, and who, after the Lady Lianne, was next in line to inherit Lord Aylion's lands and castle. It seemed that Sir Lucan believed that this cousin's highborn friends had spread rumors and told lies to arouse suspicion against Lianne, so that she might die and her cousin gain her inheritance. And that the lord bishop, who was also related to this cousin, had helped to incite the people against Lucan's lady. Sir Lucan spoke so openly of his suspicions that when he disappeared some said he had been done away with by the powerful people whom he had accused. And others thought he had ended his own life and that of the child."

Suddenly Tymmon could bear no more. Without plan or intention he jumped to his feet, one hand held up palm outward before his face, as if to ward off an attack. Seizing Troff's collar with one shaking hand, he hurried across the common room of the inn, stumbling and bumping into people and furniture in his haste. At the door he turned to look back briefly to where the stranger from Nordencor still sat alone in the darkened alcove. Then he burst out into the cold night air. Starting toward the stable, he suddenly turned again and, almost at a run, crossed the courtyard to where the stone gateposts marked the entrance to the street.

For a long time he continued to walk, with Troff trotting beside him through the dark streets of Montreff. Except for here and there where a torch burned before the doorway of an inn or the home of a nobleman, the light was so dim he could barely see the ground before him. But he stumbled on almost unaware of where he was or in what direction his feet were carrying him.

Once when he found himself before the great gates of the city he stopped, and then hurrying forward, he threw himself against the smaller inner gate. It was barred and padlocked, and when a watchman looked down from the guard tower he called up to him, "Sir, I must leave Montreff. Now. Tonight."

A second guardsman joined the first. One of them held a wineskin in his hand, and they both seemed to be in a festive mood. "Why must you leave now, lad?" one called. "It is bad luck to start a journey after nightfall. Only dead souls travel the highroad at this hour. Ghosts and demons and . . ."

The second interrupted, "What is your haste, you young rascal? Are the sheriff's men after you that you must leave the city in the dead of night? Stay where you are. We will be down to question you further."

But the steps of the guardsmen were slow and unsteady on the winding stairs that led down from the tower, and long before they reached the ground Tymmon and Troff had faded back into the darkness and disappeared in the maze of crooked streets.

They went on wandering until, little by little, Tymmon's wild thoughts calmed and his mind became somewhat clearer. At last he paused and pulled Troff to a stop beside him. "Tomorrow, then," he whispered. "We will wait and go tomorrow. And now we will go home and prepare." He looked around. In the darkness the street was unfamiliar.

"Where are we, Troff? Where is the White Boar? Take us home, Troff." Without hesitation the gargoyle turned, sniffed the air, and trotted off confidently. And it was not long before they saw ahead of them the torchlit courtyard of the inn.

Inside the familiar walls of the harness room Tymmon sank down onto his pallet and crouched forward, his arms hugging his chest as if to confine and quiet his pounding heart. For a while Troff stood beside him breathing heavily on the back of his neck and trying to lick his hidden face. At last Tymmon straightened and, taking Troff's collar in both his hands, pulled him close.

"That's why he would not tell me," he said. "It explains everything. Why he renounced his knighthood, and left Nordencor. And why he would never tell me the reason. Even after that day when he let slip that he had been born to the nobility, and even after I began to reproach him so angrily for what he had done."

Tymmon leaned forward and, putting his arms around Troff's neck, laid his head on the gargoyle's back and thought for a long time. He thought of how blind he had been to blame Komus for cruelty and even cowardice. How blind to think, as he had sometimes done, that his father had given up his knighthood because he had no stomach for bloody battle. When all the time he had acted out of the greatest bravery. The bravery to oppose, all alone, even the most powerful evil forces, as he had done in Nordencor when he accused the high lords of the court and church. And as he had probably done in Austerneve with his songs and stories and advice to the old king.

When at last Tymmon lifted his head from the gargoyle's back, he wiped his face fiercely, swallowed hard, and said, "We are going tomorrow. We are going back to Austerneve. I don't know if he is still alive, but if he is we will find him. And if he is not I will find those who took him and kill them. I will kill them, Troff. I will . . ."

Rising suddenly, he went to where his pack sat in the corner of the room and took out the Spanish dagger. Holding the gleaming weapon by its blade so that its hilt formed a cross, he knelt down below the window and held the weapon up before his face, in the manner that knights-to-be held their swords during the vigil on the night before the oath-taking. Looking up at the cross and beyond it to the dim and misty sky, he swore a solemn oath. An oath that he would not rest until he had discovered his father's fate. And that if he were no longer alive, he—Tymmon, son of Sir Lucan of Nordencor—would revenge his father's death, or die in the attempt.

He remained kneeling until his knees ached fiercely— just as a candidate for knighthood's knees were said to ache during the night of his vigil—and then he painfully regained his feet. Before he climbed into bed he turned to Troff, who had been watching his oath-taking with close attention, and reminded him to sleep well and deeply as they would be leaving Montreff in the morning.

But Troff, who usually responded to any mentioning of travel with enthusiasm, seemed troubled. Pushing his great ugly head into Tymmon's lap, he moaned softly, begging him not to be angry. And when Tymmon explained that his anger was not against him it seemed to comfort him but little. It was a long time that night before either of them slept.

Tymmon rose early the next morning. There was much to be done. After uncovering his hoard of coins from where he had hidden them under Troff's bed of rags and straw, he went first to settle his account with Harcor, the landlord.

"Well, lad," Harcor said. "I will miss you and so will my guests. But I do not fear for your future. You have a gift that will sustain you if you use it wisely."

"I know," Tymmon said, putting his hand on Troff's head.

Harcor laughed. "That gift also. But I spoke of your own talents. Farewell, then. And Godspeed."

Tymmon started away and then turned back. "Sir. The old man in the checkered coat? Has he arisen?"

The innkeeper scratched his head. "The old minstrel? He did not spend the night with us. I do not know where he has gone."

Tymmon nodded. "Well, if you see him, sir, will you tell him—tell him that Hylas of Nordencor bids him goodbye. And thanks him for—and thanks him for his message."

Later, when the shops had opened their doors, Tymmon visited the market and made several purchases. Among them were a water gourd, a supply of foodstuffs, and two new leather packs, one designed to be carried by a small donkey. Back in the stable he divided his old belongings and new purchases between the two packs. Then he called Troff to him.

He was not certain how a gargoyle would take to being a beast of burden. And in truth, when the pack was first strapped in place on his back, Troff looked at Tymmon accusingly and said that he did not think he liked it. But before long it became apparent that Troff had changed his mind and was quite pleased and proud to bear such an important responsibility.

The sun was well up into the sky on a cool clear day in late spring when Troff and Tymmon left the city of Montreff and began their journey back toward the Northern Countries and Austerneve.

THIRTEEN

T he village was called Nighmont and it lay on the highroad that led north toward Austerneve. The two weary travelers reached it in the late afternoon of their third day on the road. Days in which Tymmon had pushed ahead relentlessly from sunup until sundown.

Along the way they had eaten quickly and lightly in village markets or from the supplies stored in Troff's pack. And they had slept wherever darkness found them—in a haystack, camped in a grove of apple trees, and once, after paying three coppers for the privilege, in a farmer's drafty and rat-infested granary.

Each night before he fell asleep Tymmon took the Spanish dagger from his pack and knelt down, holding the dagger before his face, as he had done that first night in Montreff. Clasping the blade of the dagger with both hands, he renewed his oath and with it his fierce and angry resolve.

The anger was important. Without it he was only a boy, alone and almost unarmed, and sometimes fearful. But when the fire of hatred burned high and bright he became an avenger, a knight errant traveling on a holy quest to which he had sworn allegiance even unto death. But at the end of that third long day of travel, not only energy and resolve, but anger as well, were burning low.

Nighmont, like so many of the country villages, was only a collection of cob and wattle cottages straggling out from a central square, but its church at least had a whole roof, and some of the cottages were surrounded by tidy gardens. As Tymmon and Troff passed the first row of cottages an odd high-pitched but raspy voice called out to them from behind a small clump of thorn bushes.

"Hiya," the unseen presence shouted. "What be you on the rope there?"

Tymmon stopped. Although the voice had seemed to come from very near, he could see no one at all behind the small bush, which was indeed strange and more than a little unnerving. It was as if they had been hailed by some invisible creature—perhaps a restless dead soul or an evil phantom. But on the other hand, Troff was looking calmly toward the hedge and saying that it was nothing alarming.

Craning his neck, Tymmon was edging silently to the left when the voice called, "I see you. I see you sneaking at us. Run, Dalia. Run. Petrus will stop them. I got me a big stick."

Tymmon grinned. He waited a moment and then sud-

denly circled the bush, pulling Troff after him—and came
face to face with a creature so ragged and dirty that, at
first glance, it scarcely seemed to be human. But human it
turned out to be. A small and filthy creature who was, at
the moment, cringing back into the thorny bushes with a
great knobby stick raised above its head. Stringy dirt-
caked hair straggled down around a thin face, so streaked
and blotched with soil that it was almost impossible to
make out the features, except for the eyes—wide-set eyes,
the dark irises rimmed in a wide band of white, like those
of a frightened colt.

There had been someone or something else, too. Out
of the corner of his eye Tymmon had caught sight of
something small and dark as it flickered away into the tall
grass. But his attention was now fully on the one that
remained behind—who was threatening to do some serious damage with its great club.

"Now there," Tymmon said soothingly, smiling and
stretching out one hand in a gesture of peace. "We will
not hurt you. But you had best put down that club or
Troff, here, may become angry." He glanced at Troff. Actually, the gargoyle did not seem to be greatly concerned.
Sitting on his haunches, his tongue lolling, he was regarding the ragged child with calm interest.

The boy, for such he appeared to be although he was
wearing what at first glance appeared to be a tattered
gown, said nothing. But his bony face wore a frown that
was clearly meant to be of a manly ferocity. And on closer
inspection it became obvious that his only garment was
not a dress but a man's worn and ragged doublet which,
on his short and skinny frame, hung down almost to the

ground. Still brandishing the stick that was nearly as big as he was, he looked from Tymmon to Troff and back again, and then quickly away in the direction in which the smaller figure had disappeared. But then quite suddenly he dropped the club and began to pull himself free from the prickly bush.

"Coee!" he said in his strange voice, oddly cracked and rasping like that of a tiny old man. "That bush fair stabbed the life out of me." He rubbed his arms fiercely with both hands and then once more glared at Tymmon. "All your fault, too, sneaking round at us like that. Nigh scared us to death, you did."

"I am sorry," Tymmon said. "I just wanted to see who had called to me. You did call to me, did you not?"

The little boy shook his head. "No. Not to you, I dinna. Called to him there on the rope." Narrowing his eyes and stooping forward into a crouch, the boy crept nearer to where Troff was sitting. "What be ye, beastie? A lion? Nor a bear maybe?"

"A dog," Tymmon said, quickly before Troff, who seemed greatly amused, could be tempted to answer for himself. "He is my dog, Troff."

"No!" the boy said. "Truly? Only a dog, be it?" Turning, he cupped his hands around his mouth and shouted, "Come back, Dalia. There be naught to fear. It be only a boy and a great lump of a dog." Then without waiting to see if his summons was answered he turned back to Tymmon and asked, "And what be your name, boy?"

"Tym—" Tymmon began and then, "Hy—" And then stuttered into silence. He had told no one his real name since he had given it to the farmer outside of Austerneve, with such disastrous results. But somehow it felt ridiculous to give a false name to this small tattered scrap of humanity.

The little ragamuffin regarded him critically. "Doan you got a name, boy?"

Tymmon grinned. "Boy is fine," he said. "You can just call me Boy."

The child shrugged and said that Boy would do, but that he, himself, had a real name. It was Petrus, he said, and he was six or seven years old—he'd forgotten which —and he had lived in Nighmont for a long time and before that on his father's farmplace, and Nighmont was a fine village but that the country had been better, and there had been cows there and chickens and lots of milk and eggs. He had, it seemed, a great deal to say on any number of subjects. His sister, Dalia, on the other hand, who eventually came creeping back from her hiding place, appeared to be two or three years younger, and said nothing at all. They were orphans, Petrus said rather proudly.

"Orphinks," he said actually. "We be orphinks, Dalia and me. Since a long time. Since the lord's soldiers came with horses and swords and axes to take our mule away for the lord's war. Only our father tried to hide our mule so the knights deaded him, and our mother too when she tried to help him. And they would have deaded us too, only I hid us under a straw pile." He looked down at his little sister, who was leaning against him and staring up at Tymmon with dark-rimmed eyes. Huge eyes that gleamed like those of a small wild beast amid a great tangle of dirty and matted hair that hung down over her forehead.

"I'm sorry," Tymmon said. "I'm sorry that you have no . . ."

But Petrus interrupted. Shrugging, he said, "It be all right. I take good care of her. Doan I, Dalia?" He gave his sister a punch on the shoulder and she immediately hit him back with both tiny fists and then danced away out of reach. Petrus grinned. "She be a fierce one. I learn her. I learn her how to fight."

Suddenly losing interest in the conversation, he edged nearer to Troff and poked at the pack on the gargoyle's back. "What you got in there? Bread, maybe?" Putting his face close to Troff's, he repeated the question. "You got bread on your back there, Dog?"

"Not much," Tymmon said. "There was food in the pack, but it is almost gone now. I was hoping to buy a meal here in the village. Is there an inn, or perhaps a bake shop nearby?"

"Buy? You got money?" Petrus moved closer so that Dalia squeezing in front of him was almost standing on Tymmon's feet. "He got money, Dalia. To buy food with. We show you where to buy food. Dalia and me will show you."

There was, it seemed, no real inn in the village of Nighmont, but there was a house on the square where food was sometimes provided for travelers. "Mistress Ino's house," Petrus said, seizing Tymmon's hand while Dalia danced ahead of them on tiny bare feet. "We be taking you there, Dalia and me." And when they reached the square the two of them ran eagerly ahead to a stone house somewhat larger than its neighbors, and pounded on the door.

It was opened by a neatly dressed village woman, her full cheeks framed in a clean white wimple. She was smiling as she opened the door, but when she saw the two children her face hardened into a frown. Shaking a large wooden spoon in a threatening manner, she shouted, "Shoo, scat, you ragamuffins. Be off with the two of you."

The children ran, disappearing like scattered sparrows, and when Mistress Ino's attention shifted to Troff and Tymmon her anger changed to puzzled curiosity.

"Madam," Tymmon said, bowing, "I am traveling northward through your village and I would very much like to *buy*"—he stressed the word carefully—"some food for myself and my dog." As he spoke he reached into his belt, took out his bag of coins, and jingled it in his hand.

At that Mistress Ino's smile returned, and chatting pleasantly about the weather, she led the way into the cottage. Within a few short minutes Tymmon was seated before the kitchen fire eating meat pies and blood pudding. And at his feet Troff feasted on a ham bone and bread scraps soaked in gravy—not to mention a small meat pie which Tymmon slipped down to him when Mistress Ino was looking the other way.

There was, it seemed, no place to rent a room in the village, but "My husband and I own a hay barn on the outskirts," the woman said, "and for a copper more you could spend the night there. The roof is sound and the hay makes a soft resting place."

The copper changed hands and not long afterward Tymmon and Troff were on their way to the hay barn through the gathering darkness. Following Mistress Ino's directions they had just sighted the old barn, when Tymmon suddenly realized they were not alone. From somewhere behind him a small raspy voice whispered, "Did you have meat pies? Did you?" and at the same moment a tiny cold hand grasped Tymmon's thumb. Tymmon glanced down in surprise. The voice had been that of Petrus, but the hand belonged to his sister.

"Mistress Ino's meat pies be the best in the whole world," Petrus went on, catching up to trot along on the other side of Troff. "Mistress Ino's meat pies be famous. We had one once at Eastertide. Dinna we, Dalia?"

Tymmon looked down at the two small faces. In the thickening twilight he could make out little more than blurred ovals, but it would have taken a much greater darkness to hide the hungry gleam in the two pairs of eyes.

A few minutes later, and back once more at Mistress Ino's, Tymmon bought two more meat pies, started out the door, and then went back to buy another two. And when the orphans again appeared out of the darkness he gave them all four—one for each of their small dirty hands.

They disappeared then, drifting off into the darkness eating noisily. But the next morning when Tymmon awoke in a bed of soft, sweet hay, it was to look up into two pairs of eager and hungry eyes.

"Morning." Petrus was smiling broadly. Then he dropped down on his knees, crawled to where Troff still lay sprawled on his side, and whispered into the gargoyle's ear, "Morning, Dog." Troff opened one eye and grinned. And Tymmon, sitting up, rubbed the sleep from his eyes, and then sat with his chin on his knees and stared at the two small human scarecrows.

In the clear morning light they looked amazingly small, and quite unbelievably dirty, caked and smeared and blurred with soil of every color and description. Not to mention thin and hungry. Tymmon shook his head, sighed, and went on staring. An idea was forming itself inside his mind. It was a wild, foolish, and impractical idea and later he tended to blame it on Troff although he could not clearly remember what the gargoyle had actually said on the subject.

After a while he pulled his coin purse out of his belt, opened it, and peered inside. Then he thought for a while longer before he turned to Troff and said, "Not much left. We will have to try some more exhibitions."

Troff, his head cocked, rolled his eyes and agreed with far more enthusiasm than was necessary.

"I don't know how successful we would be in the small villages, but at least they might give us food. And if we stayed a few days in a larger town like Bidborn, we might earn enough to manage." He shook the purse, sighed again and, lowering his voice, went on. "I thought we had enough for the whole trip but not with four mouths to feed. And we would have to buy them something else to wear, or we would certainly be taken for beggars."

Petrus was sidling nearer, pulling Dalia after him. "What you saying about Dalia and me?" he said, his brows knit suspiciously. "What you saying about begging?"

Tymmon grinned. "I was telling Troff I was thinking of taking you with us to . . ."

Petrus jumped back, almost jerking Dalia off her feet. "No. Not begging," he said. "You not be taking us begging for you."

Tymmon grinned. "I do not blame you at all for not wanting to be beggars, but that is not . . ."

Petrus shrugged. "Oh, we be beggars, all right. Dalia and me, we been begging since our folks got deaded. But we not going to go begging for someone else again. Last harvest time a beggar lady came to Nighmont and took us to another place to beg for her. But she starved us and put lye on our arms and legs to make sores so the rich people would feel sorry for us, so we ran away and came back to Nighmont. So we not be begging for anyone else never no more."

So Tymmon tried to explain that he was not a beggar and that Petrus and Dalia would not be asked to beg if they came with him, but the children only backed farther away.

"I heard you saying about begging to Dog, there," he said, and then, narrowing his eyes even further, he went on, "And I heard you say about not enough money. How you going to get more money if you not be goin' a-begging?"

"We do not beg," Tymmon began. "We earn money by . . ." His voice trailed off as he realized that the children would not understand what he was going to say, and even if they did they would never believe it. Instead he began to prepare the packs, and when all was in readiness he slipped the collar over Troff's head and turned toward Petrus and Dalia, who were still watching warily. "Troff and I are going back into Nighmont now," he said. "If you want to come, too, we will show you how we get our money."

Petrus nodded slowly, but he moved no nearer, and all the way back into Nighmont he and Dalia followed at a safe distance. A distance great enough to prevent their being snatched and carried away to be starved and burned into professional objects of pity. Looking back at the two tiny scarecrows trudging through the deep dust, Tymmon suddenly shuddered.

"By all the saints in heaven," he whispered. And when Troff looked at him questioningly, "It is not to be wondered at that they do not believe we mean them no harm."

All the rest of the way into the village his mind was full of the horror of it, of children barely out of infancy who had already faced such terrible sorrow and need. And it was that horror no doubt that made him forget for a time that his own future was dangerous and uncertain. That he was pledged to a quest that certainly should not include two helpless children, and to a cause that left no room for pity.

Fortunately it was market day in Nighmont and the dusty square was aswarm with farmers and landholders as well as villagers. In a small open area near the booth of a tinsmith Tymmon pulled Troff to a stop. Although they had not performed since they had left Montreff, it was clear that Troff knew, and approved of, what they were going to do. The moment Tymmon raised the flute to his lips the gargoyle took his place beside him and raised his broad muzzle toward the sky. And before the first song was finished they were surrounded by an eager crowd of laughing and cheering villagers.

When Troff's songs were finished, Tymmon's solo, a lively ballad sung while accompanying himself on the rebec, was also well received, as was his brief exhibition of juggling and tumbling. But it was not to be wondered at that the villagers were most amazed and amused by the singing gargoyle. Amazed and amused even though they seemed quite ready to believe he was no more than a great, ugly dog. There was much cheering and clapping as he performed his deep bows. And when he circled among them with his pail he collected not only several small coppers but various bits of bread and cheese and other foodstuffs as well.

During the performance Tymmon had once or twice caught sight of two small raggedy figures among the audience, but later when the instruments were packed away and the crowd had dispersed, Petrus and Dalia were nowhere to be seen.

"I'm not surprised," Tymmon told Troff as they left the village and headed north along the highroad. "And it's just as well, actually. We've no right to take them with us into the danger we will probably face when we get to Austerneve. I must have been crazy to even think of it. The truth is, I just wasn't thinking. It's much better for everyone that they decided not to come with us. Don't you agree?"

Troff stopped, looked back over his shoulder, sniffed the air, and said something that could have meant yes or no.

Tymmon shrugged. Well, perhaps Troff was uncertain

whether they had been right to consider taking on the responsibility for two little orphans. But he himself was not. In fact, now that Petrus and Dalia were no longer there, staring up at him with their great hungry eyes, he could scarcely believe that he had forgotten himself so completely. He could not understand how he had forgotten the terrible nature of the quest on which he had embarked, and the vengeance he had sworn. Had even, for a short while, forgotten the anger and hatred that had burned in his heart since he had heard his father's story.

"I'll not forget again," he muttered to himself just as Troff once again stopped and, turning back, sat down in the middle of the road. Away to the south a dust cloud was rapidly approaching, and in its midst, two small scarecrow figures were racing at top speed with a stream of tattered rags flapping behind them.

FOURTEEN

"Y ou sneaked off on us," Petrus yelled, staggering to a stop in front of Tymmon and Troff. Dropping an armload of tattered and filthy rags on the ground, he clutched his heaving chest with both scrawny arms. For a moment he only gasped and sputtered, and when he once more began to shout, his funny creaky voice kept breaking into squeaks and squeals. "Dalia and me, we just gone to get our blankets and things and when we got back you gone off and left us. And you *said* you would take us with you. You be a liar, Boy."

Grinning, Tymmon cowered backwards, pretending to be terror-stricken by the violence of Petrus's attack. But then, seeing that Petrus was in no mood for game playing, he became serious. In a calm and reasonable tone he said, "But you said you would not come with me, Petrus. And I did look for you when the exhibition was over, but you had disappeared."

Still gasping and squeaking, Petrus flailed his arms, beating the air in what seemed to be anger at his own breathlessness as well as at Tymmon's desertion. "But we *told* you. We told you we be coming with you."

"What?" Tymmon couldn't believe his ears. "No, you did not. At the barn this morning you said you would never come with me, and . . ."

"That was afore we knew about how you and Dog got money by singing and"—Petrus pantomimed the playing of a rebec—"and like that, 'stead of begging," Petrus interrupted.

"But you did *not* tell me you had changed your minds. You said nothing at all to me after we got back to Nighmont."

"Well"—Petrus was still glaring but a little less fiercely —"maybe *I* did not. But Dalia did. Dalia told Dog. She told him when he come past us getting all that money in the pail."

Tymmon suppressed a smile. "Dalia told Dog—Troff? But how could she? She cannot talk. I have not heard her say a single word."

"She talks," Petrus said. "She used to talk a lot before she saw what the lord's men did to our father and mother. But now she only talks to me. Not with saying out loud, but just with her eyes, like—" He rolled his eyes expressively. Then he caught himself. "Oh! And to Dog there. Now she talks to Dog, too."

Troff was staring off to the east watching some cattle in a distant pasture, obviously pretending not to be listening, but Tymmon could see that he was grinning. When Tymmon asked him if he knew that Petrus and Dalia were planning to come with them he said yes, he did. Bouncing with both front legs in the way he sometimes did to emphasize a point, he said yes, of course, he did. But when Tymmon asked, "Then why didn't you tell me?" he only began to leap around playfully, making everyone scatter to keep from being trod upon, which meant he had no more to say on the matter.

And so it happened that suddenly, just as Tymmon was beginning to realize how lucky he was not to have two dirty and hungry little orphans on his hands, there they were. Sighing, he gathered up their worldly possessions, several ragged and dirty scraps of blankets and a few tattered shreds of clothing, wrapped them together, and tied the bundle on top of Troff's pack. Then the four of them set off up the dusty road that led toward the North Countries and Austerneve.

They camped that night beside a stream just outside the walls of Bidborn, a small town built on the top of a stony outcropping at the edge of a range of wooded hills. Before taking their evening meal from Troff's pack, Tymmon led Petrus and Dalia to the stream bank and insisted that they wash at least their hands and faces. They did so cautiously and sparingly, with Petrus complaining all the while that the water was cold and wet and was doing him serious and lasting harm. But he recovered quickly when the food appeared, and soon afterwards they both fell asleep, cuddled together in their pile of ragged blankets.

Long after the orphans, and Troff too, were sleeping soundly, Tymmon lay with his hands behind his head, thinking and planning and staring up at the branches of an oak tree as it made intricate inky splashes across the face of the moon.

He thought again, as he did every night, of the solemn oath he had sworn—to find and free his father and take revenge on his abductors, whoever they might be. And once again, as he had often done before, he tried to imagine who Black Helmet was and why he had come for Komus.

Was the huge knight in dark, unblazoned armor someone who had been angered by one of Komus's songs or stories? Or perhaps some enemy from his distant past in Nordencor? It was impossible to even guess. Only one thing was certain, and that was that the answer to the mystery could only be found in Austerneve.

But soon, with the constant sound of Petrus's wheezy breathing to remind him of problems nearer at hand, Tymmon found himself thinking more of the morrow and what it might bring. And when morning came he set his plans in motion.

"I am going into the town now," he said firmly when the first rays of morning sun touched the treetops and Petrus and Dalia had begun to stretch and yawn. "I will return soon with food and other things."

"No." Petrus struggled out of his pile of rags and jumped to his feet. "You doan go off without us. Dalia and me coming too. You doan sneak off on us again."

"I am not planning to sneak off," Tymmon said, grinning. At least he grinned the first time he said it, but as he repeated the solemn promise again and yet again he did so with growing exasperation. No matter how firmly and positively he said it, Petrus only went on glaring and would not be convinced. Not, at least, until Tymmon suggested that Troff too would stay behind.

"Oh, that be all right then." Petrus was suddenly completely reassured. "Rich people like you maybe sneak off from poor little orphinks, but not from their dog, I think. Not if they be a singing one, anyways, like Dog here."

Tymmon couldn't help laughing. "Rich people?" he said. "I am not a rich person."

Petrus rolled his eyes knowingly. "Yes, you be, Boy," he said. "We saw all those monies in Dog's pail. Dinna we, Dalia?"

Tymmon didn't bother to argue. It would have been useless, and besides he rather liked the idea that someone, even if it was only a poor little beggar, saw him as rich. So after making it clear to Troff that he must remain with the two children, he set off for the town, and when he returned some two hours later, his coin purse was empty and his pack was bulging.

"What you got there? What you got for us, Boy?" Petrus clamored as he and Dalia and Troff, too, danced around Tymmon.

"Wonderful things," Tymmon said, grinning, as he unstrapped the heavy pack and lowered it carefully to the ground. "Sausages and cheese and bread and cherries. But first we are going to do magic. We are going to change you and Dalia from two little beggars into a noble prince and princess."

What followed was nerve-racking and time-consuming, particularly the parts that involved water and soap. But at least this time the sun was bright and the air warm and dry. So Petrus's prophecies of immediate death by chills and ague lacked the conviction they had carried the night before.

Sometime later, when the ordeal was over and Petrus and Dalia stood before Tymmon scrubbed and sheared and dressed in modest but respectable homespun, Tymmon inspected them critically and thoroughly before he grinned and said to Troff, "Well, perhaps not a prince and princess, but so greatly improved I am certain their old acquaintances back in Nighmont would not recognize them. Truly, I scarcely do myself."

The soaked and scrubbed and trimmed Petrus, neatly dressed in leggings and tunic, and shod in wooden pattens, was indeed a transformation, but even more remarkable was the change in his tiny sister.

After trying for a long and painful half hour to get a comb through the tangled mat of Dalia's hair, Tymmon gave up, and using the Spanish dagger as a razor, he cut most of it away. And when what remained was thoroughly washed it sprang up into a shining cap of ringlets that framed a visage that had somehow changed from that of a small wild beast to the wide-eyed face of a human girl-child. Human, or at least partly so, for the enormous eyes, wide cheekbones, and pointed chin produced a beauty that was somehow more elfin than babylike. Dressed now in a tiny gown of blue linen, she stared down at herself, ran her hand across her shorn head, and then, looking up at Tymmon, let her lips curve upward. It was the first time Tymmon had seen her smile.

Shortly thereafter the two orphans, clumping awkwardly but proudly in their new and unaccustomed pattens, followed Tymmon and Troff up the hill and into the city.

Bidborn was a small town but obviously prosperous and strongly fortified, its high walls dropping down to sheer cliffs on two sides and protected on the others by a deep moat. Inside the walls the streets were well paved with cobblestones, and shops crowded each other along narrow streets and alleyways. Trudging along the busy streets, Petrus and Dalia stared in wonder at the two- and three-storied buildings, at the bustling crowds of people, and perhaps most of all at the many enticing wares displayed in the shops and market booths. Nudging Troff, Tymmon grinned and pointed to the entranced children.

"They've not seen anything like this before, I wager," he whispered, and Troff grinned back and agreed. Then, pulling Tymmon after him, he suddenly trotted ahead to shoulder the spellbound orphans out of the way of a passing cart.

What with shepherding Dalia past booths of shawls and ribbons and pretty toys, and Petrus past anything that looked as if it could possibly be eaten, it was some time before they reached the small hostel where Tymmon had arranged for them to spend the night. The hostel's owner, a woman of awesome size and dignity, seemed surprised and not at all pleased that Tymmon's party included an enormous dog and two small children.

"No," she said firmly several times. "You must go elsewhere. I cannot allow barking dogs and screaming children in my hostelry." But suddenly, in the midst of a third or fourth refusal, she stopped, staring down into Dalia's upturned face. For several long seconds, while

Tymmon held his breath, she said nothing at all, and when she finally continued it was to say, "There is, however, a small room off the scullery that I might let you have."

The room was indeed small, but it was clean and furnished with two well-padded cots, and to Petrus and Dalia, at least, it must have seemed a miracle of comfort. But on that afternoon there was little time to enjoy its luxuries. It would soon be sunset and there remained in Tymmon's purse only two small coppers. It would be necessary to find out at once whether the citizens of Bidborn appreciated the music of flute and rebec.

Tymmon grinned at Troff as he slipped the collar over his head and whispered, "As well as what their reaction will be to a singing gargoyle—or dog, as the case might be." Troff grinned back and said that he had no doubts—that he was certain to be a great success. And remembering the warm smiles and clapping hands in Nighmont as well as Montreff, Tymmon was inclined to agree.

"Troff and I must be off to earn our living," Tymmon said to Petrus and Dalia, who were busy playing a game that involved climbing on and off the two cots as rapidly as possible. "It would be best if you stayed here, I think."

But after some moments of thought, he changed his mind and bade the children make ready to accompany him. But it was not only the suspicious frown that was already forming on Petrus's face that caused him to change his mind. There was another reason why it might be best to appear in Bidborn as part of a family of three.

It had suddenly occurred to Tymmon that the town of Bidborn, lying as it did just outside the boundary of Unterrike, was only a few days journey from Austerneve. Although he had heard nothing in Montreff or Nighmont of the reward offered by Black Helmet, it seemed that Bidborn, so much closer to Austerneve, might well be another matter. But those who might have heard of Black Helmet's reward would have been told only to watch for a young man of thirteen summers, a wary and nervous fugitive traveling lightly and alone. Not for a young minstrel, openly performing before all and sundry and accompanied by—yes, by his younger sister and brother. Sitting both children down on the edge of a cot, he carefully explained their new family background.

"What is our father's name, then?" he asked when he had finished the lesson. "And where are we from?"

Petrus grinned triumphantly. "I know all of it," he said. "You be our brother, and we be from Nordencor, and our father's name be Lindor. Oh, yes, and your name be Hylas. And you will give me two coppers if I don't forget."

There had been no mention of coppers. "Well . . ." Tymmon was saying, when Petrus jumped down and lifted his sister from the cot.

"Don't forget, Dalia," he said, as he led her to the door. "We each get two coppers if we remember Boy be our brother and his name be Hylas. Don't forget that, Dalia."

"Hold there!" Tymmon began. "I certainly will not pay Dalia for not speaking since she never says . . ." But the two children had already disappeared into the scullery yard. Sighing, Tymmon picked up his rebec and flute and followed.

They remained in the small room off Mistress Artima's

scullery for five full days. Five days during which Tymmon and Troff performed twice daily with great success and Tymmon's purse once again grew fat with coins. But successful though their stay in Bidborn was in many ways, it was for Tymmon a busy and exhausting time.

Exhausting because—well, because of Petrus and Dalia. They had not been long in Bidborn before he realized that when he had so quickly and thoughtlessly decided to include Petrus and Dalia in his travels he had had no idea what he was doing. Having no younger brothers or sisters, he had no way of knowing the amount of time and energy that must be spent where young children are concerned. Time spent in feeding and dressing, in the buying of food and other necessities, in cleaning and grooming, not to mention in teaching and scolding. And in the case of Petrus, arguing. Arguing about everything in general but in particular about money and how it should be spent— and food and how much of it should be purchased and eaten.

The care of the two orphans certainly had turned out to be a much greater burden than he could ever have imagined, and sometimes Tymmon thought that if he had it to do over again he might not have chosen as he had. But then again, at times . . . At times such as when Petrus took on himself the role of town crier and insisted on running through the streets and squares of Bidborn shouting out the news of where and when "Hylas of Nordencor and Troff, his amazing singing dog," would next be performing. An effort which, Tymmon had to admit, had very favorable results.

And at other times when he noticed that Dalia's face

was already less pale and more softly rounded. Of course, she still refused to speak. Not even a word of the paternoster, which Petrus had learned quickly with only a little tutoring and bribing on Tymmon's part. But although she remained voiceless, Dalia's face was more and more often warmed by smiles, and when she ran to meet Tymmon with her eyes shining, he could not really wish that he had decided differently on that day outside of Nighmont.

Time rushed past, and it was not until late at night at the end of the fifth day in Bidborn that Tymmon realized that he had not thought for hours, perhaps not even for days, of his quest and of the need to hasten on toward Austerneve. He climbed out of his cot and began to dig through his pack, looking for the Spanish dagger. But when he came first upon his father's cap and bells he clutched it to his heart instead and again repeated his oath—his fierce and solemn promise to free his father or avenge his death or, if need be, to die in the attempt.

And so it was that early on the sixth day, before the sun was high in the sky, Tymmon, his faithful gargoyle, and his newly acquired brother and sister left Bidborn and set out in the direction of Austerneve.

FIFTEEN

T he highroad beyond Bidborn rose quickly toward the wooded hillside. Tymmon and his small company had been under way for little more than an hour when they found themselves among the tall trees of the Unterrike Woods. Narrower now, deeply rutted and thick with dust, the trail twisted and turned as it climbed upward. And on both sides the trees crowded down closely, amid underbrush almost as dense as that of the Sombrous Forest.

Stopping briefly to rest and eat when the summer sun was high overhead, they soon pressed on again, although Petrus had long been complaining of being tired. And Dalia, padding barefoot in the dust, her new shoes swinging in her hand, dropped down to sit in the grass beside the road whenever Tymmon allowed even a moment's pause.

It was late afternoon and the road had taken a downward turn when Dalia, who had been clinging to Tymmon's thumb, suddenly pulled on it sharply, cocked her head, and pointed to her ear. Tymmon stopped to listen.

He had just recognized the sound, the faint and far ringing of bells, when Petrus said, "Church bells. From that way. A far way off. Can we go there, Boy?"

At first Tymmon moved on, not willing to let anything change his determination to stay on the trail until the Unterrike Woods lay behind them. But when Petrus, running ahead, discovered a narrow and weed-grown pathway leading off in the direction of the faintly pealing bells, he began to reconsider.

The bells were, no doubt, ringing for vespers, which meant it would soon be sunset. And although the days were long now with twilight lasting well past compline, it was beginning to seem likely that darkness would find them still in the deep woods—a thought that made Tymmon more than a little uneasy. Fearful memories of his days and nights in the Sombrous came back to him. Lonely, hungry days, and nights haunted by fearful dreams of murderous brigands, evil harpies, and ravenous wolves.

Perhaps, he told himself, the ringing bells meant that they were near a woodsmen's village or even a monastery where they might find a safe shelter for the night. Turning aside, Tymmon led his little band of followers down the weed-grown track that wound its way into a wide wooded valley.

The bells had long since ceased to ring when the trail at last leveled off and broke free of the woods at the edge of a wide meadow. And at the far end of the open land, rising up from the flat valley floor, was a manor house. So tall and narrow it resembled an enormous tower, it was built of pale gray stone and fortified with crenellated battlements at the four corners. Tymmon stopped to stare in wonder and surprise.

The sun was low now and a thick ground fog lay across the valley floor. The lower walls of the towering manor were wrapped in mist, so that it appeared to be floating on a cloudy island. But higher up, still touched by sunlight, its pale gray turrets stood out in sharp contrast against the dark green of the wooded hills.

"Look." Petrus was on tiptoe with excitement. "A castle. It be a real castle, bean't it, Boy?"

Tymmon couldn't help smiling. To a child who had spent all his days in a country village and had never seen a real castle such as Austerneve or Unterrike, this turreted manor house would indeed seem to be castlelike. "Well, not exactly," he told Petrus. "But it is a noble and beautiful manor. I remember my father saying that such homes, far from cities or towns, often welcome travelers because they bring news of the outside world, and"—he grinned at the gargoyle who, head cocked, was listening with interest—"sometimes entertainment. Perhaps they will let us sing for our supper, Troff."

A few more yards down the rutted and overgrown roadway and they were themselves enveloped in the swirling gray fog. Rolling banks of heavy mist, like phantom sea waves, poured over them, blurring their vision and making distances difficult to judge. As they walked steadily forward, the towering gray walls seemed to loom near, recede, and then approach again. But at last Tymmon looked down to see the worn planks of a drawbridge under his feet, and as he did so he was suddenly aware of a damp and rotten stench that arose from the stagnant water of the moat.

He had no more than set foot upon the bridge when Petrus, who had been running ahead, stopped suddenly and came back, his eyes wide.

"What is it?" Tymmon asked.

Petrus stared at Tymmon and then turned to stare back toward the house, and as he did so his sister tugged at Tymmon's hand and made a strange trembling sound. Not a word, but more like the cry of a frightened newborn animal.

"What is it, Petrus?" Tymmon said again, more urgently.

Petrus sidled nearer and grasped Tymmon's other hand. "I doan know," he said. For a moment he stared up into Tymmon's face and then turned to look back over his shoulder. A shudder lifted his thin shoulders. "I doan know," he said again, and then plaintively, "Where be the people, Boy?"

"The people?" Now that it had been brought to his attention it did seem odd that they had as yet seen no one. No riders coming in from the fields and forest, and no watchmen on the walls. But there were, of course, possible explanations. "Why, I suppose they are all at vespers, or eating their evening meal," Tymmon said. "Come along. We will see the people soon enough."

But no one hailed them from the gate tower as they made their way across the drawbridge, the sound of their footsteps on the planks echoing hollowly in the deep silence. The inner doors of the house, heavy wooden panels, strengthened by bars of intricately wrought iron, were closed and bolted. A basket of wilted flowers sat on the threshold, and just above it a bell rope hung down within easy reach. As Tymmon's hand touched the rope, a strange sound from Troff made him pull it back quickly, as if it had burned his fingers.

It had not been exactly a growl. It had been, in fact, more like a whimper—a sound that one would not expect to hear coming from so fierce a creature as a gargoyle. Troff was backing away, his bat-wing ears held close against his head and his tail down between his legs. Petrus and Dalia looked from Troff to Tymmon, and their large eyes were full of fear.

Tymmon tugged at the gargoyle's collar. "Come now, Troff," he said briskly. "What ails you?" But Troff only continued to pull away. Reaching up quickly before he could be dragged out of reach, Tymmon seized the bell rope and pulled hard. And from somewhere far away a bell pealed faintly.

Tymmon dropped the cord and the sound faded away into silence. But it was a different silence now. A stillness that moved and trembled, full of sounds not heard but only echoed from somewhere deep within. The sounds of a restless stirring. Of seeking eyes and listening ears. Of the reaching out of many hands, and the vain and voiceless movement of pale lips endlessly repeating cries for help and mercy that had not been heard.

Seizing the children's hands and whispering to Troff to come away, Tymmon turned and ran. Ran frantically up the hill until, out of the mist, a figure appeared directly before them, blocking the path to the road above.

It was a woman, an old, bent woman, wrapped in a hooded gray cloak, carrying in her arms a great bundle of starburst wildflowers. Tymmon was still staggering backwards in surprise and fright when she spoke.

"May God bless you, pilgrims," she said. And then stretching out a trembling hand toward Dalia, "And bless you, little one, for your tears."

Dalia was indeed crying. Crying without a sound, but with a flood of tears that overflowed her huge eyes and ran down her face in gleaming pathways.

Still badly shaken, Tymmon reached out to where Troff was standing beside him. With his hand on the wide, warm back he asked, "Troff?" and the gargoyle said the woman was not harmful. Nothing else. Just that she meant no harm.

It was Petrus who spoke to her first. "Where be they, mistress? Where be the people?"

As she turned to answer, her hood fell back and Tymmon saw the she was not ancient as he had thought. Not old, at least with years, but only empty and lifeless as a burnt-out hearth.

"They are there," she said, looking up toward the high walls of the manor. "They are all there. Each of them where they will ever be. The young lord at the entryway with his sword beside him, my lovely lady where she fell on the grand staircase, and the old lord Dannold before the hearth in the great hall. They are all there, in the places where the baron's men found them. In the halls and passageways, in the kitchen and scullery. And in the nursery." Her voice faltered, and reaching up she pulled her hood down over her face and stood silently with her hand across her mouth. When she at last dropped her hand and lifted her eyes, she looked first at Tymmon.

"I had cared for them since they were born. If I had only been there I might have hidden them. I might have hidden at least one of them. But I had gone off to visit in the village." She broke off again, and again there was a long pause before she turned to Petrus and Dalia. Curving her lips into the shape of a smile, she reached out to touch their heads.

"Pretty children," she said. And then with her eyes again going dark with memory, "Such pretty children they were." Pulling two large white starbursts from the bundle in her arms, she held them out, one to Dalia and the other to Petrus. "Pretty children," she said again.

She passed by then and continued down toward the manor house on slow unsteady feet. Standing close together, motionless and silent, except for a sobbing from Dalia, they watched her make her way down through the drifting fog. They went on watching as she emptied the basket of dead flowers into the moat, filled it with fresh ones, and placed it before the barred doors. Then she knelt, and crossing herself, she began to pray.

Tymmon prayed too. And as he prayed to the Holy Mother for mercy, he heard Petrus loudly and fervently saying the paternoster, the only prayer he knew. From Dalia there was only the soft sobbing, but when the praying was over and Tymmon turned to go, she shrugged his hand from her shoulder and began to run down the path. Before the barred doors she dropped down beside the kneeling woman and placed her flower on the doorsill beside the others. A moment later she was back clinging to Tymmon's hand.

They hurried on then, for a time almost running. They reached the highroad and pressed on through the gathering shadows. And then, just as Tymmon had feared, they found themselves still deep in the Unterrike Woods as twilight began to fade into a moonless night.

As he had done in the Sombrous, Tymmon built a campfire and stacked near it wood enough to last until dawn. Troff was restless, sniffing the air and listening to every sound, eager to go off on a hunting expedition, as he had done in the forest. But Tymmon did not want him to leave.

"There is food enough in the pack for tonight," he told the gargoyle. "And before tomorrow is over we should be on Austerneve land and among farms and villages. Stay here with us tonight."

So Troff agreed and satisfied himself with bread and sausage, and when they had all eaten, they spread their blankets beside the fire. But for a long time Tymmon was unable to sleep.

He could not sleep because he could not close his eyes without seeing again things he did not want to see, the silent valley, the mist-shrouded manor, and the haunted eyes of the old-young nursemaid with her prayers and flowers. And other things not really seen but that now arose in clear and sharp detail before the eyes of his mind —a once young and lovely lady who would lie forever at the foot of a grand staircase, an old man sprawled in death before a fireplace, and bloody handprints on an open door through which could be seen the cradles and toys of a nursery. At last he stopped even trying to sleep and, wrapping his blanket around his shoulders, sat with his chin on his knees and stared into the fire.

He had not been sitting there for long when Dalia came to sit beside him, and soon afterwards, Petrus.

"You could not sleep either?" he asked, and they nodded and moved closer. Troff, too, changed his position, crowding in to sprawl across Tymmon's feet. For a long while they remained silent, even Petrus, and when at last he did speak it was only to say, "Talk to us, Boy. Tell us about something far away and a long, long time ago."

So Tymmon began to tell them about when he was a child—"as old as you are now, Petrus." He told them about Mistress Mim, the shoemaker's wife, who had been his nurse when he was very young. How she had fed and clothed him and taught him his prayers, since Komus, who taught him everything else, was not one for much praying.

"She sometimes scolded Komus—Lindor, I mean—for not teaching me to pray, and sometimes for letting me run wild all day playing at war with Lonfar. But Kom—my father, didn't really let me run wild, at least not all the time. When he was free—when he was not needed by the king—he spent much of his time with me, teaching me to read and write, and sing and play the flute and rebec."

It had been a long time since Tymmon had allowed himself to remember fully those early simple years when he had been proud to be the son of the wonderfully talented minstrel and court jester of Austerneve. But now that he had begun, the memories kept flooding back.

Memories of games played with his father. Complicated riddling and guessing games that continued sometimes for days at a time. And miming games, too, in which they took it in turns to silently imitate some citizen of Austerneve, while the other tried to guess who was being impersonated.

Leaping to his feet, Tymmon began to imitate, in just the way Komus had done it, the castle's chief cook, waddling around the kitchen sniffing and tasting, and slapping any unlucky scullery maid or water boy who happened to get within reach.

When he had returned to his place by the fire, Petrus said, "And did your father teach you to hunt, too?"

"To hunt?" Tymmon said, puzzled, before he remembered that, according to his own telling, his father, Lindor of Nordencor, was supposedly a huntsman.

"Oh, yes," he said. "Of course he taught me to hunt. Hunting, of course. But my father was a man of many talents and he taught me many other things as well."

Petrus nodded. "Do I get two coppers if I remember all the things he taught you?"

Tymmon shook his head, smiling ruefully. "You could not possibly remember all the things he taught me. He taught me—so much. Things that I am only now beginning to understand myself."

"Hmmm," Petrus said, thoughtfully. And then after a moment, "Why does he have two names? Sometimes you call him Komus."

"Do I?" Tymmon said. "I suppose it was only a slip of the tongue."

"Hmmm," Petrus said again. "Do I get two coppers if I forget that sometimes his name be Komus?"

They both laughed. "Go to sleep," Tymmon said. "It is very late, and we must be on our way early in the morning."

The children returned then to their own blankets, and after he had built up the fire, Tymmon did also. But now when he closed his eyes he no longer saw the manor house and its horrors. Instead there was Komus impersonating the cook, and then Lord Bumpplon, the fat and pompous chief councilor to King Austern. And then, dimly seen through approaching dreams, he watched Komus's imitation of Father Nominus, the doddering old priest, who often went to sleep in the midst of masses and other rituals. And then Tymmon, too, went fast asleep.

SIXTEEN

B y midmorning of the following day they were nearing the outskirts of the Unter-rike Woods. The trees were smaller here and grew less densely. Now and then, when the high ground sloped more steeply, it was possible to catch a glimpse of the open land of the valley below.

It was Troff who was first aware that something was approaching. Pausing suddenly, he turned his huge, blunt-snouted head to the left and then to the right, sniffed the air, and made a warning noise deep in his throat. Then Tymmon heard it, too, a deep rhythmic pounding, the sound of an approaching horse, running at top speed.

Grabbing the children's hands, and calling urgently for Troff to follow, he retreated up the hill to where a clump of saplings offered cover. Among the bushy young trees he crouched, pulled the others down beside him, and waited, his heart pounding.

The thundering beat grew louder and with it another familiar sound, or pattern of sounds. The squeak and clink and rattle of an armed and armored knight riding at full gallop. It was a sound well known to any who, like Tymmon, had been an eager observer at a great many jousts and tournaments.

"What be it," Petrus whispered, tugging at Tymmon's elbow.

Tymmon had no more than answered "A knight. It is a knight—on horseback," when the horse burst into view and bore down on them at top speed. A huge thick-chested bay, wild-eyed and heavily lathered with sweat, and on his back a rider in richly ornamented armor—who had clearly lost all control of his enormous steed.

The horse, his mouth twisted open and his massive neck bowed against the pull of the reins, charged down the hill while the shining knight, off balance and with one foot out of its stirrup, bounced and clattered and shouted curses. But the runaway held his course, straight toward a great oak tree with wide spreading branches.

Tymmon was wincing and ducking his own head in anticipation of what was to come when the rider's helmet met a low-hanging limb with a resounding clang. A sound quickly followed by another metallic thud and clatter as the heavily armored body hit the earth. The horse continued on and soon disappeared into the valley, his thundering hoofbeats fading away to nothing. Silence returned. The fallen knight lay perfectly still and made no sound at all.

For several moments Tymmon's group sat frozen, staring at the fallen warrior in horrified surprise. Then Tymmon rose to his feet and with the others close behind him —Troff sniffing noisily and Dalia whimpering with anxiety —made his way down to the scene of the accident.

The knight lay flat on his back with one leg twisted awkwardly beneath the other and with his arms thrown out on each side. His suit of armor was, indeed, richly decorated and fashioned in the latest style. It was also clearly very new with no sign of rust or wear, and with none of the dents and nicks such as were often acquired in repeated wars or tournaments. No dents except, of course, for a deep crease that now ran across the helmet just above the visor, where the oak tree's branch had struck.

On the breastplate a coat of arms was richly inlaid with gold and silver, depicting in its center the figure of a rampant griffin, half eagle and half lion.

Tymmon gasped. It was the coat of arms of the baron of Unterrike. And this poor victim, possibly dead or dying, might well be the baron himself or his son, the baronet Quantor, the young lord who had been living in King Austern's court and to whom Lonfar was pledged as squire. Except that Tymmon remembered the baron as being much too heavily built to fit into this particular suit of armor. And the baronet, who would still be in service at Austerneve, would not likely be riding alone here in the Unterrike Woods. But whoever it was, it was clear that he was in desperate need of help.

Bracing himself for the sight of a terrible bloody

wound, Tymmon reached out, touched the gleaming helmet, and then carefully lifted its visor.

There was no blood. And the youthful face, comely at first glance but somehow lacking in form and structure, was not that of the baron, nor of the baronet. The palely lashed eyes were tightly closed, and except for the large discolored lump on his forehead, the young knight might have seemed only to be peacefully asleep.

"Be he dead, Boy? Be the knight dead?" Petrus was on his hands and knees, with his nose only inches from the opened visor.

"I do not know," Tymmon said. Pushing Petrus back, he leaned forward and placed his ear close to the mouth and nose of the unconscious man. Then he shook his head. "No. He is not dead. At least not yet. I can hear him breathing."

Beside him, Dalia let out a quavering sigh of relief. Then she poked Tymmon and pointed down at the twisted leg.

"Yes," Tymmon told her. "You are right. Here, Petrus. Lift the other leg while I try to straighten this one."

With the twisted leg in a more natural position, Tymmon sat back and tried to decide what else it might be well to do. At first he could think of nothing, and for several minutes the four of them, Tymmon and Troff on one side and Petrus and Dalia on the other, sat quietly around the body like mourners at a wake.

But then Tymmon noticed that the flare at the rear of the helmet caused the knight's head to be tipped forward in what would surely be an uncomfortable position. After lifting the visor and unbuckling the neck strap, he removed the entire helmet and again revealed the pale, pudgy face. And the whole head as well, where stiff blond hair escaped around the edges of a heavily padded hood. The lump on the forehead was darkening, but now the lips were moving slightly, and the eyelids twitching.

Freeing the head seemed to have been successful, so the injured leg came next. As Tymmon removed the sabaton, a foot covering of overlapping plates, he gave it to Dalia for safe keeping, and handed the greave, the guard for the lower leg, to Petrus. Then he examined the leg. Even through the padded leggings and silken hose the swelling was apparent. He was touching it gently, feeling for a break, when the knight moaned sharply and opened his eyes.

He stared first at Tymmon and then at the two children. Then he raised his head, bellowed something unintelligible but clearly threatening, moaned loudly, and clutched his brow.

Tymmon waited until he released his hold and again opened his eyes. "Sir," he began, "I fear you are gravely . . ."

"My sabaton. What are you doing with my sabaton?" the knight shouted at Dalia. "Put it down, you little thief."

And when Tymmon again tried to explain that he and the others were only trying to help, he was again interrupted by angry shouts. It took some time before Tymmon was able to complete his message. Indeed, it might have taken far longer if it had not been that the fallen warrior's shouts clearly were causing tormenting pain in his wounded head, so that each bellow was followed by a moment of anguished silence. It was only into these momentary hushes that Tymmon was able to offer his message that no one intended to steal anything and that they only wished to be of help.

At last the young knight ceased to bellow and regarded Tymmon with silent suspicion while he began to explain how he and his family had happened by "just as your lordship's horse came charging down . . ."

At the mention of his horse the young man again began to curse and shout. "Where is he? Where is that son of Satan? Bring him here! I'll beat him to a bloody pulp! I'll cut out his treacherous heart and . . ."

At that point he again clutched his head, and in the silence that followed, Tymmon was able to say that he could not fetch the horse as he had long since disappeared, and to ask if there was anything else that his lordship would like him to do.

At first the young man could not decide. The knight— who soon announced himself to be Lord Wilfar, youngest son of the baron of Unterrike—gave an order, and then changed his mind. His first demand was for Tymmon's party to go at top speed to Unterrike to fetch help. But then, as they were preparing to obey, he suddenly revised the order.

"Once out of my sight you'll likely only fetch back some older members of your thieving tribe to slit my throat and steal the rest of my belongings. No. You will stay with me. All of you. You will help me to make my own way back to the castle."

But after his first attempt to gain his feet, he reverted to the first plan, and then once again changed back. It was not until an hour at least had passed, and much preparation had been completed by Tymmon, that the decision was final, and the procession was under way.

First came the young knight, stripped now of all his gleaming armor. Leaning on a long staff on one side and Tymmon on the other, and with his injured leg bound and splinted, he managed to hobble forward with much groaning and swearing. He had, however, refused to part with his sword: strapped around his waist, the gem-encrusted scabbard flopped to and fro, constantly whacking Tymmon's shins as they lurched forward.

Behind this stumbling pair followed Troff and the two children, whose progress too was slow, burdened as they were by various bits and pieces of armor. The breastplate and backplate hung across Troff's back over his already heavy pack. Petrus wore the dented helmet, at first with some pride and pleasure, and carried various pieces of leg harness. Even little Dalia struggled along under the weight of brassards and gauntlets. Crippled and heavily laden, the little caravan moved forward in fits and starts.

They rested first in the shade of an old elm. Leaning back against the tree trunk, Sir Wilfar drank from Tymmon's water gourd, drank again, and then leaned back limply and closed his eyes. Petrus and Dalia squatted nearby and stared at their new traveling companion with open curiosity. Troff had collapsed some distance away. He seemed anxious, aloof, and watchful. But when Tymmon came to him and removed his burden of pack and armor, he grinned and quickly rolled on his back, offering his stomach for a scratch.

"Hey, old friend," Tymmon whispered, "what do you

think? Will it be wise for us to go to Unterrike? It is very near to Austerneve, you know."

The gargoyle's only answer was to ask for more scratching, but later, when Sir Wilfar opened his eyes, frowned at the children, and told them to move away, Troff clearly said that he did not like the young knight. And Tymmon grinned and said he felt much the same. "But I suppose we must help him on a little farther. Perhaps we will soon meet some of his people, and then we will be allowed to continue on to Austerneve."

Tymmon went back then to sit near the injured knight. A number of questions had occurred to him, and when Sir Wilfar opened his eyes, he ventured one of them.

"How is it, sir, that you were riding alone and in full armor so far from your castle?"

The question aroused more oaths and mutterings, but then an answer was forthcoming. "I had decided to leave early for the tournament, before the rest of my father's party had finished their everlasting preparations. I wanted to arrive early to accustom my new horse to the lists—curse his evil heart—and to be the first to register my name, that I might get my choice of the contenders' pavilions. My squire and I left before the others and took the faster route through the foothills, but we had not gone far when the faithless wretch deserted me. He was riding behind me and I did not realize that he had gone until it was too late. I went back to look for him but he had disappeared."

Tymmon was aghast. Such behavior in a pledged squire violated the oath of loyalty, one of the most sacred charges of chivalry. "Why would he do such a thing? Are you sure he was not silently ambushed by brigands or . . ."

"No. He deserted," Sir Wilfar said and then went on to give his reasons for thinking so. His faithless squire, foisted upon him for political reasons it seemed, was the heir to a nearby estate. The spoiled and pampered only son of some minor noble, he had from early on been surly and resentful. "And today when I disciplined him by bringing my riding crop down across his shoulders he muttered something rebellious, and it was shortly thereafter that he disappeared. I will see to it that he is charged with treason, and also with endangering my life."

"Endangering your life?" Tymmon asked.

"Yes, indeed. It was only because of my anger when I realized that I had been deserted, that I reacted as I did when Avenger shied at a shadow and almost unseated me. In my just and understandable wrath I forgot for a moment that the beast's trainer had warned that he would bolt if he were beaten over the head, and I . . ." He shrugged.

"I see," Tymmon said solemnly, hiding the smile that might have given away his sudden conviction that the steed, Avenger, had cleverly made use of an oak tree branch to live up to his name.

"And now I will miss the tournament at Austerneve and my first opportunity to gain fame and glory in the lists. And it is all the fault of . . ."

He rambled on but Tymmon had ceased to listen. "Austerneve?" he asked. "There is to be a tournament at Austerneve?"

"Yes. To celebrate the betrothal of my brother,

Quantor, to the princess Amica, King Austern's granddaughter and heir."

"Princess Amica?" Tymmon gasped in disbelief. The small pale child he had often seen in the great hall at Austerneve, who even now could not be more than eight or nine years of age.

"Of course she is still quite young," Sir Wilfar said as if in answer to his thoughts, "but the wedding will not take place for some years, and in the meantime . . ." He grinned, and silently Tymmon supplied what he was obviously thinking. In the meantime the baronet would be recognized as the legal heir to all the lands and holdings of Austerneve.

It was a short time later, while he was strapping Troff into his pack and armor, that Tymmon noticed that Sir Wilfar was watching him with some interest. And it was when they were again under way, stumbling slowly down toward the road that could now be seen in the valley far below, that the knight began to ask questions about the gargoyle.

"What breed is he?" he asked. "I have seen dogs of similar shape and conformation in the low countries, but none quite so large and of such a striking appearance. You should outfit him with a spiked collar and enter him in the dogfights in the villages. One could win a small fortune with such a dog if he is as fierce as he looks."

And when Tymmon said he did not know the name of the breed but that he understood it was one developed for the hunting of bear and boar, the knight's interest seemed even keener.

"And is your dog trained for hunting, then?" he asked.

"He is a great hunter," Tymmon said proudly, and then, watching the eager gleam in the young knight's eyes, he suddenly wished that he had said no, that Troff was entirely useless as a hunter and as a fighter as well.

On the rest of the journey there was no more talk of Troff. Instead Sir Wilfar began to describe his recent knighting. As they stumbled forward with the large and well-fleshed youth leaning heavily on Tymmon's shoulder, he spoke at great length of the glories of knighthood and of the inspiring ceremony that had so recently raised him to that exalted level.

He told of the fasting and bathing that had preceded the long night's vigil kneeling in the deserted church, and then of the glorious oath-taking before the assembled nobles. He went on then to tell of his high hopes for fame and glory since he was obviously so well suited to knighthood. Well suited to join the ranks of the loyal and courageous men who loved honor above all else and welcomed bloody battle as the most noble and glorious of all conditions of life.

They had almost reached the highroad and Tymmon, exhausted as much by Sir Wilfar's tongue as by the weight of his body, was no longer making much response, when a sudden question sprang to his lips unbidden.

"Sir Wilfar," he hastily inserted into a momentary pause, "do you know of a deserted manor house about a day's journey to the south in the direction of Bidborn?"

"A deserted manor?" Wilfar repeated. And then, "Oh, yes. In a valley below the highroad? A tall structure with towers at the four corners and built of pale gray stone?"

"Yes," Tymmon said. "That is the one."

Sir Wilfar chuckled. "It is Unterrike property now," he said. "It was once held by the family of a minor noble known as Dannold, but it is now part of Unterrike, fairly won in honorable combat."

"Fairly won in honorable combat?" Tymmon whispered. "Were you there, sir, when Dannold Hall was taken?"

"Was I there?" Wilfar said disgustedly. "No, I was not. I very much wanted to be, but that was some two years ago, before my knighting, and my father refused to let me ride with him and Quantor. But I have since been with him on other dangerous undertakings. I have . . ."

"But, sir," Tymmon interrupted, "I thought the High King had outlawed such private battles. I thought . . ."

Wilfar laughed. "The High King is far away and he seldom hears of such small misunderstandings between neighbors. And even if he should, my father has heard that a gift of suitable generosity can turn aside his anger."

Tymmon staggered, shaken by a flood of violent emotions, and Sir Wilfar cursed his awkwardness. At that moment the injured knight came very close to being unceremoniously dumped on the ground and left to fend for himself. In fact he surely would have been had there not been a sudden shout from Petrus.

"Look. Look, Boy. An army. Down there on the road."

It was true. Far down on the valley floor an army, or at least a large procession of horsemen, had come into view on the low road that led to Austerneve. At least a dozen knights in full armor led the party, followed by thirty or forty squires, pages, and other attendants. Up and down the column banners fluttered and the sunlight glinted off shining armor, gem-encrusted satins and velvets, and the sleek hides of well-groomed horses. And behind the procession a great column of dust rose up from under the horses' hooves and drifted backwards like a following white cloud.

It was, no doubt, a glorious and stirring sight, but at the moment Tymmon was too troubled and harassed to appreciate it. On the one hand Sir Wilfar was dragging him down the steep hillside yelling and shouting, while behind them Dalia was shrieking in wild hysteria.

But although Wilfar and Tymmon staggered downward as fast as they could and the young knight's shouted summons seemed loud enough to alert an entire kingdom, no one from the passing army looked up or answered. Deafened, no doubt, by their own clanking, jangling, clopping progress, they seemed to hear nothing, and soon passed from view, hidden by their trailing cloud of dust.

Tymmon broke away then and ran back to comfort Dalia, who had collapsed in a moaning, trembling heap.

Petrus crouched over her, vainly patting her back. "It be the army that frighted her," he said. "It be like the one that came to our farm. Just like that one."

Sitting beside Dalia, Tymmon pulled her onto his lap and cradled her while he told her over and over again that the army had meant them no harm and that they were now gone away.

By then Sir Wilfar, who had necessarily remained where Tymmon had left him, had begun to shout for him to return. Again Tymmon considered going off and leaving the knight to find other rescuers as best he might, but in the end he relented and returned with a suggestion.

"I'm afraid, sir, that we can go no farther as we are. As you can see, the path below us becomes much steeper. But perhaps I could send Petrus down to the road to stop the next travelers and ask them for assistance."

Wilfar considered the proposal suspiciously for some moments before he agreed. But agree he finally did. And so it was that before another hour had passed Petrus had stopped an ox cart and enlisted the help of a farmer. A large and muscular farmer who lifted the young knight onto his back like a sack of flour and carried him down to his cart.

And soon afterwards Tymmon, Troff, and the two children were packed into the ox cart along with Sir Wilfar and his arms and armor. And the cart was on its way back toward the south and the Castle of Unterrike.

SEVENTEEN

Tymmon had not meant to go to Unterrike. Once Sir Wilfar had been safely settled in the ox cart, along with his ankle-bruising sword and all his various bits and pieces of armor, Tymmon had bidden him and the farmer good-bye and Godspeed. But as he took Petrus and Dalia's hands and turned toward the north, the knight called to him.

"Halt, lad," he said in a surprisingly pleasant tone of voice. "Do not go. I would like you to accompany me back to the castle. I want to"—there was a brief pause—"to reward you for your assistance. Yes, I wish to repay you for coming to my aid. Here. Climb up on the cart and we will be off. And your dog, too. And, yes, the children as well, I suppose. Bring them all up into the cart. There is room enough for all."

Tymmon was declining the kind offer with humble and

grateful thanks when Sir Wilfar ordered the farmer to lift the children into the cart. And when the huge man had obeyed without hesitation, and when neither the farmer nor the young knight paid the slightest attention to Tymmon's protests, there was nothing for Tymmon to do but join them, and Troff with him. The driver climbed onto his seat and cracked his whip, the oxen plodded forward, and before an hour had passed the walls and towers of Unterrike rose up on the horizon before them.

The Dark Castle, as Unterrike had long been called, was built of stone the color of old ash heaps. Looming up against the sky from its base on a rocky hillside, its crowded throng of ashy-hued towers and turrets made it seem a city of darkness. And well it might, since for many years, long before the reign of the present baron, the castle had figured in the darkest dreams of all its neighbors.

It was not Tymmon's first visit to Unterrike Castle. Some years before he had been there with his father. It had been at the time that the treaty of peace had been renewed between Austerneve and Unterrike, and all of King Austern's court had been invited to join in a celebration at the baron's castle. And as a favorite of the old king's, Komus had been granted the right to bring his young son to witness the grand and glorious occasion.

And now as the ox cart slowly climbed the approach road, Tymmon's mind was full of recollections of that other visit. Memories of how, even then in the midst of what was intended to be a joyous celebration, there had been for Tymmon at least a constant feeling of vague and distant threat.

He remembered how, although great fires roared night

and day in dozens of huge hearths, he had often shivered in the chilling drafts that came and went throughout the castle like long shuddering sighs. And how at times he had seemed to hear a deep and silent lamentation, as if even the dark stones of the castle walls were given to weeping.

Now and then during the long, slow ride Tymmon wondered with some uneasiness just why they were being taken to the castle. He did not really believe it was just to reward them for their help. Had Sir Wilfar's intention been only that, he could easily have given Tymmon a few coppers or even, if he felt extraordinarily grateful, a piece of silver.

There was the possibility that the young knight knew about Black Helmet's reward and had guessed Tymmon's true identity. But on further thought, that seemed rather unlikely, since Sir Wilfar obviously had so little interest in who Tymmon might be that he had not even bothered to ask his name.

Catching Petrus's eye, Tymmon smiled, remembering that Sir Wilfar had asked no questions about Petrus or Dalia either, so it had not been necessary for Petrus to remember that he was Tymmon's brother. He had, in fact, asked no questions at all—except about Troff.

Tymmon's mind was busy with the possibility that Troff had something to do with their visit to Unterrike Castle when the cart crossed the long drawbridge and passed through the imposing gateway. Once inside the walls it rumbled across the intricately tiled courtyard, past grand facades with pointed-arch entryways and beautiful traceried windows.

While Petrus rose to his feet and gasped and jabbered with excitement, Dalia climbed into Tymmon's lap and clung to him tightly, staring with wondering eyes. Only Troff seemed unimpressed by either the grandeur of their surroundings or by the novelty of a ride in an ox cart. Lying with his great head resting on his paws, he seemed entirely unconcerned, his eyes barely open below the wrinkled folds of skin on his bulging forehead.

With the courtyard behind them, they continued on up a sloping passageway, through the gate to the inner keep, and stopped before the magnificent entrance to the baron's palace. As the ox cart labored to a stop, huge copper-plated doors swung open, a crowd of excited servants appeared, and Sir Wilfar was immediately lifted up by many hands and carried away. And soon afterwards Tymmon and the others were surrounded and ushered into a long narrow room, the great hall of Unterrike Castle.

Carrying Dalia, and clinging to Troff's collar with the other hand, and with Petrus clinging to the back of his tunic, Tymmon was swept into the hall in the midst of a flock of servants who then disappeared and left them standing alone. Not far away a large woman in a long, loose kirtle with flowing fur-trimmed sleeves, and wearing on her head an elaborate cone-shaped headdress, was bending over Sir Wilfar, who lay sprawled among an avalanche of pillows on a high-backed bench.

Sir Wilfar was talking, as usual. The lady listened, now and then looking back over her shoulder at Tymmon and his little group. At last she turned and beckoned to them, smiling graciously, but at that moment several more people entered the room and she hurried to meet them.

The newcomers, an important-looking gentleman in a long dark robe and four servants in brightly colored livery, clustered around Sir Wilfar. The dark-robed man examined the injured forehead and then the swollen leg thoroughly before he directed the servants to lift the young knight and carry him from the room. The lady followed them to the door of the great hall and then, as if suddenly remembering, hurried back to where Tymmon waited.

"Welcome, children," she said in the high, quavering voice that was often used by noble ladies. "My son, Sir Wilfar, has told me that you came to his rescue when he was injured and alone. He wanted to speak further with you immediately and to reward you for your helpfulness, but the doctor has ordered that he be immediately put to bed and treated for his injuries. He will send for you tomorrow. In the meantime . . ."

The lady turned toward the distant doorway, where a servant in beautiful braid-trimmed livery stood at attention. A tall, dignified man, stiff with dignity and self-importance, he was obviously the head chamberlain or someone of similar rank. Motioning for him to approach, the baroness told him that "these children and their dog are to be taken to the kitchen and fed, and then housed in one of the unused servants' rooms in the kitchen wing. See that they are well fed, and that the dog is given his fill of fresh, raw meat. My son particularly asked that he be fed fresh, raw meat."

She turned back to Tymmon. "I will not see you on the morrow as I will be leaving at dawn in the caravan that will take those of the court who do not ride a-horseback to the celebration at Austerneve. But my son will send for you when he awakens, which, I must warn you, will not be early, as he is generally a late riser. But he asked me to tell you that after he has seen you, you will be free to go."

Somewhat relieved, Tymmon had started toward the door when behind him he heard the baroness speaking to the chamberlain. "See that they are taken good care of, Roscall. Particularly the dog. His lordship seems to have taken quite a fancy to the ugly beast. I believe he intends to add him to his kennel of fighting dogs."

He knew it. It had been Troff all along that had caused Sir Wilfar to insist on their accompanying him to the castle. As the head chamberlain led the way through many magnificent rooms and then down one long corridor after another, Tymmon clutched the gargoyle's collar and wondered what a knight so ready with the whip and sword would do if he were refused something he badly wanted. It was a frightening thought. But there was some comfort in the fact that Troff did not seem frightened.

Padding along with his nose only inches from the velvet breeches of the chamberlain, who glanced back at him uneasily from time to time, Troff seemed to be thinking only of amusing himself by making the haughty head servant nervous.

He is not worried because he knows I would never sell him, Tymmon thought. No matter what, I would never part with him.

After being generously fed in the servants' kitchen, while a flock of spit turners, scullery maids, and other young kitchen laborers watched in awe as Troff devoured most of a raw leg of lamb, Tymmon's company was taken to their room. Led by a young understeward carrying a tall candle, they left the kitchen by way of the scullery and wound their way down two flights of stairs. The air had gone cold and dank, and Tymmon was thinking that they must be well down into the bowels of the earth, when the servant stopped and opened a door.

The room was cold and windowless, but it was furnished with a table, a bench, two large pallets, and plenty of heavy blankets. The steward took another candle from his satchel, lit it, and placing it on the table, announced that they had better not leave the room in a mess, and then disappeared. The door had scarcely shut behind him when Troff and the two children were sound asleep, and it could not have been much longer before Tymmon, too, was deeply unconscious.

He had not expected to sleep. Worried as he was by Sir Wilfar's plans for Troff, he had intended to only warm himself beneath the blankets while he planned a strategy for the day ahead. A way, perhaps, to convince Sir Wilfar that Troff would be useless to him as either a hunter or as a killer in the village dogfight arenas.

But the day had been long and extremely strenuous and Tymmon had not yet arrived at any plan when his thoughts swirled and blurred, and he was sound asleep.

It was several hours later that he was jolted awake by a familiar but entirely unexpected sound. Troff was singing. The candle on the table, much lower now, was still burning, and by its light Tymmon could see that Petrus and Dalia had also been awakened. Sitting up on their pallet, they were staring at Troff with surprise and amusement. Meanwhile the gargoyle sat on his haunches near the door and, with his head thrown back, was crooning his most mournful lament.

"Dog be singing," Petrus said unnecessarily. "Why be Dog singing, Boy? He waked us up."

"He woke me up, too," Tymmon said. He got out of bed, crossed the room, and squatted down before the gargoyle. "What is it, Troff?" he asked. "Why are you singing now?"

But the singing went on and on . . . and then suddenly Troff dropped his head, licked his chops, grinned at Tymmon, and began to scratch a flea. Tymmon went back to bed.

But he had no more than pulled up the blankets when the singing began again, livelier now, and with a faster beat.

"Troff," he said, irritated now. "Stop it. You will awaken all the servants. Stop, I say."

But the singing continued. At last Tymmon jumped up and, grabbing the gargoyle by his muzzle, forced his jaws together. And it was in the following silence that he heard it—the sound of faraway music. Too faint and indistinct for the tune or even the instrument to be recognized, but definitely music. Pushing past Troff, Tymmon seized the latch and opened the heavy door. Now the sound was much clearer. Still distant, but clearly . . .

"Boy," Petrus said. "That be yours. That be one of your songs."

Tymmon stood perfectly still, as if some great force had passed over him, jolting his mind and body into immobility. He tried once, twice, and a third time before his voice responded and he was able to say, "No. It is one of my father's songs."

Stepping out into the pitch-dark, tunnellike hallway, he listened, cupping his hand behind his ear. The song was coming from the left. Behind him Troff was beginning to sing again. Back in the room, Tymmon again closed the gargoyle's mouth and then, snatching up the candle, set off down the hall following the sound of the flute.

But of course he was followed. He had gone only a few yards when he realized that Troff—and the children, too —were close behind him. He stopped, thinking to order them back to the room, but looking down into Petrus's eager eyes he quickly realized that there was no time for the argument that would follow such an order. So they went on, the four of them, along a stretch of narrowing stone-walled passageway and then down a flight of circular steps.

The music grew louder as they went, and once or twice Troff began to sing, but he stopped quickly when Tymmon put a warning hand upon his muzzle. They were nearing an intersection where two long tunnels crossed when the music stopped.

"It be gone," Petrus whispered. "The song be gone, Boy." He glanced nervously over his shoulder. "Maybe we best go back?"

"No," Tymmon whispered. "No." He moved on more slowly, waiting—until, just as he had hoped, the music began again. Another slow, sad tune but now even more loud and clear.

They passed by two more intersections and then down another stairway. Down and down into a narrower tunnel, where the air smelled of mildew and the walls oozed moisture.

The music was very near now, and up ahead a glimmer of light appeared and grew brighter. They turned a corner and came suddenly upon a gate. A great barred gate made of strong iron poles set in a metal frame. Beyond the gate an oil lamp burned brightly in an alcove, and beneath the alcove a man sat slumped forward over a table, his head on his arms. Near the sleeping man's hand, a large ring of keys lay on the table.

As Tymmon peered between the bars of the gate the music ended, broken off in mid-phrase, and it was then that he noticed another barred gate to the left of the sleeping man. A series of iron bars—and behind them something was moving. A figure was moving toward the gate, and then a face appeared between the bars.

It was a thinner, paler face, and heavily bearded now, but the eyes were still the same, dark-lashed and wide-set beneath arching brows—and still alive with sharp intelligence and, at the moment, shocked surprise.

Pressing his face between the bars, Tymmon fought back a need to scream or shout so violent that his throat ached from the effort. Fought back all sound—and silently mouthed the word "Father."

Komus's finger flew to his lips, signaling silence. For a brief moment he stared at Tymmon, shaking his head in amazed disbelief, and then his eyes turned quickly toward the sleeping dungeon keeper. He grinned his old double-edged grin and then, pointing to the sprawled figure, pantomimed drunkenness, crossing his eyes and dropping his jaw. It was not until then that Tymmon noticed the wine-skin that lay on the floor beneath the table.

"The keys," Komus mouthed, miming the turning of a key in a lock.

Tymmon nodded. Putting an arm, a leg, and a shoulder between the bars, he tried desperately to force his head through. But the space was far too narrow. But as he gave up and extracted himself, he noticed that Petrus was try-ing too. Tymmon held his breath as the little boy man-aged to get half his body between the bars—and then, just as with Tymmon, his head stopped his progress. He tried frantically, and Tymmon tried to help, grasping the small head and turning it this way and that, to try again from another angle.

Tymmon was still pushing and Petrus was protesting not quite silently that he was in pain, when a soft voice whispered, "Doan hurt Petrus. I can do it," and Dalia squeezed easily between the bars, tiptoed on tiny bare feet to the table, slowly and silently raised the ring of keys, and returned with them to where Tymmon waited with out-stretched arms. And it was not until much later that he realized that she had spoken.

There followed a long period of nerve-racking tension as Tymmon tried one key after another—and finally found the correct one. The key turning in the lock grated slightly and the iron gate squeaked on its rusty hinges, while Tymmon held his breath in anguished dread. But although the flat-faced dungeon master mumbled when the key turned, and snorted and turned his head when the hinges squeaked, his eyes stayed closed.

Only a few seconds later the door to Komus's cell was

opened and Komus was grasping Tymmon by his shoulders and then clutching him to his chest, as silent tears ran down his cheeks and Tymmon's also. They were still standing there crying and laughing silently, or almost silently, when a sudden growl from Troff warned of danger.

Tymmon whirled in time to see the dungeon keeper rising unsteadily to his feet, his eyes fixed in dull wonder on the small crowd that now clustered in Komus's cell. The blank eyes focused with difficulty, blinked and focused again, and then the man's hand went to the hilt of a broadsword that hung from his waist. He had unsheathed the heavy weapon and was starting forward when Troff charged.

With an angry roar the gargoyle crossed the anteroom at full speed and flung himself on the guard, striking him in the chest. They went down heavily, with a thud and a great clatter, as the sword flew backwards and struck the wall. And then, as Troff stood over him growling softly, the guard moaned, twitched, and then lay still.

Tymmon and Komus were still frozen in shocked surprise when Petrus, with his usual interest in fateful happenings, joined Troff beside the fallen guard. Putting his ear near the man's mouth, as Tymmon had done with the unconscious knight, he listened and then sat up to announce, "I think he be dead, Dog. I think you deaded him."

But Petrus's diagnosis proved to be premature; the guard was already beginning to stir as Tymmon and Komus carried him to Komus's cell. There, after binding and gagging him with strips of blanket, they left him behind the locked cell door.

In the guards' room, Tymmon had already gathered the children and was starting toward the outer gate, when Komus called to him, "Come with me, Tymmon. We may need your help," and led the way down a narrow passage. They passed one cell and another, and then Komus stopped and unlocked the door of the third.

Inside the tiny enclosure a man wrapped in a blanket was sitting on the edge of a hard, bare bench. A young-old man with a long tangled beard, haunted empty eyes, and trembling hands. At first Tymmon thought him to be a stranger, and a hopelessly mad one, far gone into living death. But he was wrong. When Komus laid his hand on the man's shoulder and said, "Can you stand, Prince? We have come to take you home," the prisoner's eyes lit with understanding and he struggled to his feet.

And Tymmon's mind reeled as he recognized King Austern's son, Prince Mindor, who had been taken by brigands three long years ago and long since given up for dead.

EIGHTEEN

I t was not until they had crossed the dungeon guardroom, passed the outer gate, and started up the first narrow passageway that a question arose that had no immediate answer. The question was asked by Prince Mindor, and it was immediately clear that everyone, including Komus, expected Tymmon to supply the answer.

In his raspy voice, creaky with disuse, the prince asked, "Where are we going?"

Tymmon realized that he didn't know. After some moments' thought he shook his head. "It must be past midnight now," he said. "We cannot leave the castle grounds at this hour. The gates are certain to be closed. I don't know how . . ." He stopped to think. "But the gates will be opened early tomorrow to permit the passage of a wagon caravan."

"A wagon caravan?" Komus asked.

"Yes, a ladies' cavalcade," Tymmon said. "Taking the ladies of Unterrike to—a celebration." He glanced at the prince and decided against mentioning that the festivities would be in honor of the betrothal of his little daughter to the baronet Quantor. Instead he forced his mind to turn to the possibilities that might be presented by the crowds and excitement of the caravan's departure.

"There will be a great bustle and . . ." he began, and Komus took up his thought. ". . . much confusion. A swarm of excited noble ladies and their even more excited maids and attendants. Besides a great throng of common folk, no doubt, who will come to goggle and gossip. Yes, if there is any chance of passing through the gates unnoticed it would be at that time. But where are we going at the moment, Tymmon?"

"Well," Tymmon hesitated. "I don't . . ."

"You seem uncertain," Komus said. And then, smiling, "But your noble friend does not."

Following his father's glance Tymmon saw that Troff, who had gone on ahead, was now looking back impatiently.

"Yes," he said. "He thinks I do not know the way back to the room where we were staying when we heard your flute and . . ." But that was a long story. For the moment Tymmon returned to the question at hand. "And in truth I am not sure I do know the way. We came down many passageways. But Troff will know. Take us back to our room, Troff." He again moved forward. "Come. We must stay somewhere until daybreak, and the room will be as safe a place as any."

So Troff set off leading the way, down passageways and up flights of stairs, passing intersections confidently that might have fooled a less keen-nosed guide. Trotting along sharply, he stopped now and then and turned back to wait as the rest of the party followed more slowly. First Petrus, carrying the dungeon keeper's lamp, with Dalia beside him. And then Komus supporting the weak and shaky prince on one side while Tymmon steadied him on the other.

As they moved cautiously forward, Tymmon found himself given to bone-shaking shudders that came and went and came again, especially when he let his eyes turn to the left, to the pale, bearded face of the prince. The noble prince, so long ago given up for dead, but now here beside him, clutching his arm and leaning heavily against his shoulder. And to an even deeper quaking that shook him so hard he almost forgot to breathe when his eyes turned even farther, to where his father met his glance and grinned at him in the same old mock-the-devil way.

Before they had gone very far Komus whispered, "How is it that you are here, at Unterrike, Tymmon? Did you guess that I was here?"

Tymmon shook his head. "No. No. I did not guess at all. I was on my way back to Austerneve to search for you when we stopped here, but I did not dream that you were here." He started, then, to tell about Sir Wilfar and about why he and Troff and the children had been in the Unterrike Woods—and then gave up.

"It is a very long story," he said. "Perhaps it will do for now to say that we were here only by accident, and we were planning to leave tomorrow. Until we heard your flute. Or that is, until Troff heard it." He glanced at the flute that hung around Komus's neck by a leather cord.

Komus shook his head in amazement. "You would have left without knowing, except that you heard the flute," he said wonderingly. "So the flute has truly saved my life. It was a gift from one of the dungeon guards. Not the drunken gentleman who is now resting in my cell, but another, more sensitive, soul. I told him he saved my life by giving it to me, and now that seems a greater truth than I knew. Without it I might well have lived for scores of years and then died in that godforsaken hole."

"But why?" Tymmon asked. "Why were you in the baron's dungeon?"

"I was abducted by the baron and . . ." Komus had begun when Tymmon gasped.

Black Helmet. Black Helmet was the baron of Unterrike. Now that he had heard the words, it seemed that he had always known it. The thick-bodied, harsh-voiced man in the shrouded armor could not have been anyone else. "But what—what did the baron want of you?"

"He took me because he knew that I had been trying to warn the king against him. That I was trying to prevent him from stealing Austerneve by guile, since the High King had forbidden the use of force in such endeavors. Prince Mindor and I have discussed it many times since we met here in the baron's luxurious hostelry just three months ago. Prince Mindor was taken by a band of Unterrike knights disguised as brigands, in order to rob King Austern of his rightful heir. And I, to stop my warnings about the heir the baron had in mind to replace him on the throne of Austerneve."

The prince nodded and agreed, but Tymmon was already away on another thought. "But why me? That night in the tower they were trying to take me also."

"Yes, they tried and failed. And how *did* you manage to escape them for so long? I see that I have raised a son of matchless artfulness and cunning," Komus said. And then before Tymmon could start to answer, "Another long story, I suppose. But the answer to your question—why they also wanted you—is simple enough. The baron's original plan was not to imprison me but to force me to become his advocate in court. To make me, whom they knew to be a trusted friend to King Austern, into a supporter of all of Unterrike's schemes and purposes. Which I would do because it would be you, Tymmon, who would be held hostage, under threat of death if I failed in any mission they set for me to do. But when they could not find you they kept me instead, reasoning that if they could not have me as a supporter, they would at least keep me from being an opponent."

A bloodcurdling thought came to Tymmon and he started to ask, "But then why, when they couldn't find me, didn't they . . . ?"

He stopped as Komus interrupted. "Why did they keep me alive? I, too, have asked myself that question. As well as why they kept the prince alive. I do not know, really, except that the baron is a cautious man. I believe that he likes to have a second plan on hand to fall back on in case his favorite evil scheme does not develop properly. He must have had other possibilities in mind for the prince and me also."

As they moved slowly forward, Komus continued to

make comments and ask questions. He asked in particular about Troff and the children.

"And your companions, Tymmon?" he asked. "This noble band of warriors who have overcome dungeon walls and iron bars to free the Dark Baron's most important prisoner. I would dearly love to know where and how you managed to recruit such an army. Or would adopt be a better word for it?"

And again Tymmon began to explain, and then because of breathlessness brought on by emotion as well as the effort needed to support the badly sagging prince, he said that he would explain it all later. "But for the moment"—he smiled at his father across the prince's drooping head—"I have heard you say, Father, that one makes many new friends when one travels. And I have been on the road for more than three months."

Komus returned his grin and said, "God be praised you were not wandering for an even longer span. You might well have returned with a dozen children for me to father, as well as an untold number of enormous four-legged beasts."

At that Petrus, who had been walking just ahead, turned and, walking backwards, said to Komus, "Be you our father now, sir? 'Cause Boy be our brother." He looked at Tymmon slyly. "See, I dinna forget. Your name be Hylas, except when it be Tymmon, and me and Dalia be your brothers."

And then Dalia said clearly and distinctly, "I be a sister, Petrus. Girls be sisters," which caused Tymmon to stagger in astonishment. And it was only then he remembered hearing the same small voice say, "Doan hurt Petrus. I can do it." Tymmon was still staring at Dalia, speechless with surprise, when Troff stopped suddenly before the door of the servants' room that they had left less than an hour before.

Back in the small room, while the children huddled beneath blankets on one pallet and the prince on another, the thinking and planning went on. The prince, although seemingly gaining in alertness and understanding with every moment spent outside his cruel, dark cell, was still alarmingly weak and frail. The three long years that he had been held in the dark and cold of the dungeon had robbed him of all his former strength. Getting him out of Unterrike Castle and then across the long miles to Austerneve was going to present a multitude of difficulties and dangers.

Their only chance, Tymmon thought—and Komus agreed—would be to start at earliest daybreak and make their way into the narrow alleys that wound among the jumbled and crowded tenements of the castle's laborers. There they would wait until the courtyard filled with crowds awaiting the departure of the caravan. And then among laborers, merchants, and beggars they would wish the departing ladies Godspeed and, in the meantime, work their way down to and through the great gates. It was a dangerous plan but, it seemed, the only possible one.

The eastern sky was barely beginning to lighten when Tymmon's company, which now included two thin, ragged, and bearded men, made its way through the sculleries and pantries. There was no point in strolling casually here in order to suggest innocence. Strangers seen to be wandering inside the palace walls before daybreak would cause immediate suspicion, no matter how innocent their bearing. Like a herd of wolf-threatened deer, they stopped to listen before every doorway and then scurried to the next.

Their luck held. The huge kitchen was still uninhabited, the outer door to the vegetable scullery was bolted only on the inside, and the servants' courtyard was empty. But once outside the inner keep their behavior changed. Now they could no longer hope to avoid being seen, so they had to rely on being seen but not noticed.

Here on the poor streets inhabited by palace servants and laborers, some early risers were already up and about. Grooms passed on their way to the stables, no doubt to prepare the caravan's many horses. Bakers stoked their ovens and peddlers prepared their wares for the crowds that would soon be gathering. Now Komus and the prince walked apart from the others, pretending to be what they greatly resembled, two notably unsuccessful beggars, while Tymmon and his family followed a few yards behind.

Tymmon's group moved slowly, stopping at food shops to stock their packs, and at booths and shops to pretend to examine the wares. And then they moved on, always keeping the two ragged men in sight. And by the time the sun had cleared the horizon they had joined a growing crowd in the palace courtyard.

The caravan was now being assembled in front of the palace doors. The first four wagons, richly painted, fitted with padded benches, and covered by elaborately decorated canopies, were obviously vehicles prepared for the comfort of noble passengers. These were followed by several open transports which would carry not only servants but also a great number of trunks and clothespresses. And beyond the palace, in the passageway that led to the stables, a mounted escort was gathering, a troop of men-at-arms that would accompany the caravan to protect it from attack by brigands or other dangers.

As the noble ladies in their elaborate headdresses and richly embroidered gowns finally began to make their way down the grand staircases to be helped up into the high-slung wagons, the thickening crowd pressed forward, staring eagerly. In the general excitement Petrus and Dalia seemed to have forgotten for the moment that they were fugitives, and let themselves be caught up in the general enthusiasm of the other spectators.

But Tymmon, although he tried to play the role of curious commoner trying for a glimpse of the grand life, was far from being at home in the role. As he moved his little party through the crowd, inching always toward the great gate, he was constantly watching for danger. For curious or suspicious eyes, or for a search party of palace guards, who might by now have found the imprisoned dungeon keeper, and have set out to find the escaped prisoners and their rescuers.

The loading of the wagons seemed to take forever, but at last the first driver cracked his whip and the procession began. And as the glittering cavalcade moved forward, the crowd followed, thinning itself in the narrow passageway and, in the outer courtyard, spreading out into a great sea of bobbing heads and jostling shoulders. Tymmon, with Dalia riding on his back and with one hand clutching Petrus and the other gripping Troff's collar, pressed forward in the midst of the crowd, his head swiveling constantly as his eyes and ears strained to catch the approach of danger.

Near a buttress on the left side of the great gate he pulled his party to a stop. There they waited until the final horsemen cleared the gate and set off down the road. Set off down the open highway followed by a number of the most determined of the spectators, who continued to follow for some time, waving kerchiefs and shouting "Godspeed" and "Safe journey."

It was not until Tymmon had seen two ragged figures stumble through the gate and disappear into the heavy plume of dust, that he led his party out under the heavy drop gate. Under the gate and then on across the drawbridge, expecting every second to hear a cry of "Halt" or the rattle of pursuing footsteps.

But there was no pursuit. Not there on the drawbridge and not later as they trudged through the thinning dust, moving ever nearer to the two ragged beggars. And not throughout that long, exhausting morning, as once again they joined into one company, left the roadway, and set out over the rolling foothills that lay between Unterrike and Austerneve.

By then they had almost ceased to worry about human enemies. There was a new threat now to their further progress, the prince's increasing exhaustion. At last, not long after they reached the beginning of Austerneve land, it became obvious that he could walk no farther. They spread a blanket for him in a sheltered spot under a low wind-twisted oak, and when he was resting comfortably, Komus charged Tymmon with his care and went on alone.

They waited an hour and then two, while Tymmon bathed the prince's face with water from the gourd, and coaxed him to eat a little water-softened bread. And Dalia sat beside him and talked to him softly and steadily in her sweet newborn voice. Long afterwards the prince told Tymmon that it was Dalia's voice that had given him the strength to go on living through that long afternoon. Dalia's voice and the sunshine, which he had not seen for three long, dark years.

And then Komus returned with a farmer and donkey cart. A farmer that Komus had not lied to about the possible danger from Unterrike pursuers, but whom he had exhorted into a great fever of patriotism for Austerneve and its ancient royal family. Exhorted and charmed and captivated as well, as only Komus could charm and captivate. So that the farmer had gladly left his fields in the midst of a day's work and joined the dangerous rescue of King Austern's heir.

Much later, just as dusk was thickening into darkness, the donkey cart passed through the great gate of Austerneve, into a castle that was soon to be shaken by the most joyous celebration that the ancient kingdom had ever known.

EPILOGUE

T ymmon was looking for his flute. It was a quiet morning. The first really quiet and uneventful morning, in fact, since the return to Austerneve, and he suddenly felt the need for music. He knew the flute was still in his old pack, and that the pack had to be somewhere in the rather disorderly suite of rooms that made up their new quarters. But he couldn't remember exactly where he had put it.

Their new home was in the palace proper and had been, until quite recently, occupied by the baronet Quantor and his staff. But now the baronet had been, along with all the Unterrike nobility, stripped of his rank and sent into exile by command of the High King. And the baronet's suite was the new home of Komus and his family. The grand and palatial home of Komus, the one-time court jester who had recently been given the title of

Honored Councilor and High Chamberlain to the court of King Austern IX.

The suite included several large and elegant rooms that were, at the moment, crammed with pieces of furniture and other objects, not yet organized into any sort of useful unity. There were, for instance, various belongings salvaged from the old room in the northwest tower, as well as many pieces left over from the baronet's household. Plus all the magnificent furnishings and works of art newly lavished upon Komus, and Tymmon too, by the grateful king. Not to mention the lovely and valuable sculpture of the Holy Mother which had been presented to Tymmon with great ceremony by another thankful father—Sir Hildar.

For a moment Tymmon's search was forgotten as he remembered with great satisfaction the visit from Lonfar and his father. How Sir Hildar had requested an audience with the new Honored Councilor and his son, Tymmon, whose brave deeds had exposed the evil deeds of the Unterrike knight to whom Lonfar might, all unknowingly, have pledged himself. He could recall most of the grand words in which Sir Hildar expressed his, and his son's, humble thanks for what Komus and Tymmon had done, and how Komus responded gravely, with only a small twinkle in his eyes, that it had all been Tymmon's doing. And how Lonfar had fidgeted, and blushed, and then, at his father's urging, had muttered, "My humble thanks also."

Tymmon grinned. It was a recollection he knew he would enjoy for years and years to come. But for now he reluctantly forsook such pleasant memories to return to the task at hand—the unearthing of the old pack that he vaguely remembered storing away somewhere amid all this elegant clutter.

He had already examined the grand drawing room where Petrus, Dalia, and Troff were engaged in a noisy game that seemed to have no particular wins or losses, but involved a great deal of running and shrieking—and good-natured growling on the part of Troff.

And now Tymmon was searching a room that contained only a beautiful desk of inlaid wood, a table, some chairs, and a number of cabinets and clothespresses.

He smelled the pack before he saw it. On opening a large cabinet with ornately carved double doors, he was immediately aware of an unpleasant odor that seemed to be coming from under a pile of decorative wall hangings. And under the tapestries he found his pack.

The smell, he found, was the product of a very old and moldy pork dumpling. A dumpling that had been purchased from a peddler on the morning of the escape from Unterrike and, in the score of days since, had been quietly rotting away among the precious objects that had been Tymmon's only possessions for a long and desperate time.

Holding his nose, Tymmon inspected the dumpling, which seemed to have sprouted a furry coat and turned an interesting shade of green. Then he lifted it gingerly between thumb and forefinger and crossed the room with considerable haste, to where an open window overlooked the fosse. As the dumpling splashed into the inner moat, he wondered briefly if such an overly ripe offering would offend the king's fat and fussy fish. Then he went back to the table, pulled up a chair, and began, slowly and solemnly, to bring forth his long forgotten treasures.

First came several articles of clothing, sturdy doublets, gaiters, and jerkins, purchased in Montreff after his fortunes had begun to change for the better. They were not, of course, raiment of the fine quality to which he was now becoming accustomed, but they were of well-woven homespun, and smelled only slightly of rotted dumpling. Tymmon folded them neatly and placed them carefully to the left of the pack.

Digging farther, he next found, wrapped in an old doublet, the flute and rebec. Placing them on the other side, Tymmon went deeper, unearthing the knife, the ax, the tinderbox, and various lengths of rope. Objects that for a lonely and frightened fugitive had made the difference between life and death. Handling them with grateful respect Tymmon arranged them neatly across the table in order to honor them with the serious consideration that they so richly deserved. It was not until then that he found the two remaining objects, hidden under a layer of rags at the very bottom of the pack. The Spanish dagger and Komus's cap and bells.

He was still sitting at the table sometime later, deep in thought, when he heard footsteps and then a series of sniffs.

"What in God's name is that dismal smell," Komus said. "Something is dead, if I am not mistaken. A rat, perhaps?"

"No," Tymmon said, grinning. "Only a dumpling. But it has departed now. Flown out the window."

Komus pulled up a chair and sat down. "Another long

mysterious story, I suppose. Well, I am ready. Begin the telling."

So Tymmon explained about the pork dumpling and then went on to point out the other items the pack had held, and to explain each one's significance. Tymmon had long since given his father an account of all his adventures, but he had only touched lightly on the time spent in the Sombrous Forest. But now he spoke in detail of the cold and hunger and the constant fear of wolves and other dangers. Komus listened carefully, from time to time nodding his head in understanding and then shaking it in wonder.

"It is amazing," he said when Tymmon's story was finished. "Amazing that you survived such a pilgrimage, and not only survived but flourished. And rescued not only the prince and myself from living death, but two children as well. Tymmon, you are truly . . ."

His voice broke and he shook his head, as if unable to say more, but when he did speak again some minutes later, it was to utter words that Tymmon had never in his lifetime thought to hear.

"Tymmon," he said, his voice grown suddenly solemn, "I have been thinking about your noble heritage—our heritage in Nordencor. I long ago swore a solemn oath never to return to that accursed city, or to renew my acquaintance with the ones I once called friend or kinsman. But now I have come to feel that I did indeed wrong you in making such a choice for you also. And I know that after you learned of that choice you felt betrayed and cheated of your birthright. And now—" He paused, running a slender, long-fingered hand through his curly hair.

"I am sure now that if we went to King Austern with our story he would help in any way he could to enable you to claim the lands and titles that are yours by right of birth." He smiled wryly. "You would be late in entering into your training for knighthood. But not too late, I think, for one so experienced in such knightly deeds as rescuing princes in distress. Not to mention various and sundry others, less noble, but equally in need of deliverance."

Feeling a desperate need for air, as if a great drowning wave had rolled over him leaving him gasping for breath, Tymmon staggered to his feet and hurried to the window. The tears in his eyes made the sun seem to dance on the water of the fosse and turned the roses in the garden beyond into flames of red and gold. He stood there for an unmeasured time before he came back to his place at the table. Across from him, Komus sat quietly waiting with the strange painful smile still on his lips.

"About my future, Father," Tymmon said. "I have been thinking." He reached out and pulled two objects toward him—the Spanish dagger and the cap and bells. He lifted the dagger first, the beautiful and costly weapon that might well have been given to a young knight at the time of his entry into knighthood. Turning it slowly in his hands, he let the sunlight from the open window turn it into a thing of deadly beauty.

" 'Tis true that I have long dreamt of knighthood. But recently I have been thinking of other things. Of things I have seen and learned on my"—he paused and smiled—"pilgrimage. And of what I would someday hope to be." He reached out with the other hand and picked up the cap and bells. Making a scale of his two hands, he weighed the dagger against the cap. Then he smiled at Komus and widened his eyes as though in surprise as he let the cap sink down as though its weight was much greater than that of the dagger. "And see how the scale has tipped. I think now that I would prefer to be a court jester, Father, if I could be such a one as you have been."

"Truly," Komus was saying, "have you thought carefully of . . ." But at that moment Troff trotted into the room. He came first to Tymmon, nudged him, and sighed, rolling his eyes back in the direction of the drawing room. Then he plodded across the floor to where sunlight was pouring in through the window and collapsed.

"He says the little savages have worn him out," Komus said.

Tymmon looked up sharply. "Did you hear him say . . ." he began and then stopped. In all the days and hours since they had been reunited Tymmon and Komus had talked of many things. Of almost everything. But there was one subject that neither of them had ever mentioned. Komus had not spoken of Tymmon's mother, the lady Lianne, or even so much as mentioned her name, although he had listened, stone-faced and silent, to Tymmon's telling of what he had learned from Jarn, the jongleur, of her life and death.

And Tymmon had not told his father of his belief that Troff was an enchanted creature and of how they were able to speak to each other.

But now Tymmon said, "He speaks to me, Father. Not as much now as he did when we were alone in the forest, but he still tells me very clearly what he is thinking and—" He was silent for a moment before he went on, grinning to show that he was giving his father permission to laugh at what he was saying. "When he first came to me in the forest I believed him to be a magical beast, a gargoyle enchanted into life. But now . . ."

But Komus was not laughing.

"Lianne talked to animals," he said. And then he added, "Your mother, Tymmon."

Tymmon nodded. "I know. Jarn told me. And you once spoke of it too. Of one who talked to animals, although you did not say her name or that she was my mother."

Komus's eyes were blank and inward. "She called them messengers sent from heaven."

Around a tightness in his throat Tymmon said, "Jarn did not tell me that." He searched his father's face, seeing the deep and bitter pain, and the courage that had made him able to hide it beneath songs and jests. After a while a new thought came to him and he asked, "Do you believe that Troff—was sent to me?"

And then Komus, who had always said he believed in very little that he had not seen for himself, said simply, "Yes, I think that is true."

"Sent to me by—by heaven?"

"Perhaps. Perhaps by one who now dwells there."

"And do you think Troff really talks to me, Father?" Tymmon's question was hesitant and uncertain, because sometimes he was not sure that he himself believed it.

Komus grinned and called to Troff, who quickly roused himself, trotted across the room, and laid his great ugly head upon Komus's knee, peering up at him from under his wrinkled brow. And Komus scratched behind the batwing ears and said, "I would be a poor fool, indeed, if I did not have the greatest faith in the voice of this enchanted monster."

Then he handed the flute to Tymmon and, taking up the rebec, strummed a chord and said, "Come. Let us hear that voice again."

They played and sang together for a long time.

ZILPHA KEATLEY SNYDER has written many distinguished books for children including *The Egypt Game*, *The Headless Cupid*, and *The Witches of Worm*, all Newbery Honor Books and American Library Association Notable Books for Children. Her most recent books for Delacorte Press are *Libby on Wednesday*, *And Condors Danced*, and *Janie's Private Eyes*, this last an addition to the author's several well-known novels about the Stanley family.

Of *Song of the Gargoyle*, she says, "High among the periods that inspired my childhood dreamscapes were the middle ages. Not a very specific or historic middle ages, actually, so much as a fantasy world peopled by beautiful princesses and—most especially—by noble knights. I especially liked the knights. No doubt due, at least in part, to the fact that they rode horses. (I was also enamored of cowboys.) However, when I grew older and less romantic, I began to look at my hardware-clad heroes from a more critical point of view. Knights, I discovered, were often a pretty cruel and bloodthirsty bunch, not to mention ignorant and superstitious. Besides which, they probably smelled bad. So when I got around to setting a story in their time, I cast about for a hero or two with a better odor. And the result was Tymmon and his father, Komus. And Troff? Just another tribute to the memory of various more-or-less-miraculous four-legged friends."

Zilpha Keatley Snyder lives in Marin County, California.